"Too much too soon, Allison?"

Nelson murmured, his green eyes narrowing as they met hers.

"Please," Allison said, flustered, trying to move away. He held her firmly.

"You're twenty-five," he said solemnly. "Too old for little-girl games."

"Gene," she protested breathlessly.

He bent toward her. "Yes, it feels good, doesn't it?" he breathed, pride and faint arrogance in the way he was watching her. "You're very, very aroused, Allison," he said softly. "And just so you won't forget until I see you again…"

She gasped, shocked and frightened by the intimacy.

He lifted his head, frowning. "My God," he breathed. "You don't think I meant to hurt you?"

"Di-didn't you?" she whispered shakily.

"I'm not a gentle lover," he finally said quietly, searching her eyes. "I've never had to be. My kind of woman can match my passion move for move, and it's always been rough and wild because I like it that way. But next time," he whispered against her lips, "I'll be less wild with you. The last thing I want is to make you afraid of me."

She swallowed hard. "I'm not afraid."

Diana Palmer got her start in writing as a newspaper reporter and published her first romance novel for Silhouette Books in 1982. In 1993, she celebrated the publication of her fiftieth novel for Silhouette Books. *Affaire de Coeur* lists her as one of the top ten romance authors in the country. Beloved by fans worldwide, Diana Palmer is the winner of five national Waldenbooks Romance Bestseller awards and two national B. Dalton Books Bestseller awards.

DIANA PALMER

NELSON'S BRAND

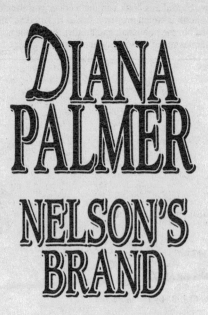

Silhouette Books

Published by Silhouette Books

America's Publisher of Contemporary Romance

SILHOUETTE BOOKS

ISBN 0-373-48361-9

NELSON'S BRAND

Books by Diana Palmer

Silhouette Romance

Darling Enemy #254
Roomful of Roses #301
Heart of Ice #314
Passion Flower #328
Soldier of Fortune #340
After the Music #406
Champagne Girl #436
Unlikely Lover #472
Woman Hater #532
*Calhoun #580
*Justin #592
*Tyler #604
*Sutton's Way #670
*Ethan #694
*Connal #741
*Harden #783
*Evan #819
*Donavan #843
*Emmett #910
King's Ransom #971
*Regan's Pride #1000
*Coltrain's Proposal #1103
Mystery Man #1210

Silhouette Books

Silhouette Christmas Stories 1987
"The Humbug Man"

Silhouette Summer Sizzlers 1990
"Miss Greenhorn"

To Mother with Love 1993
"Calamity Mom"

Montana Mavericks
"Rogue Stallion"

Abduction and Seduction 1995
"Redbird"

A Long Tall Texan Summer 1997

*Long, Tall Texans
‡ Most Wanted Series

Silhouette Desire

The Cowboy and the Lady #12
September Morning #26
Friends and Lovers #50
Fire and Ice #80
Snow Kisses #102
Diamond Girl #110
The Rawhide Man #157
Lady Love #175
Cattleman's Choice #193
The Tender Stranger #230
Love by Proxy #252
Eye of the Tiger #271
Loveplay #289
Rawhide and Lace #306
Rage of Passion #325
Fit for a King #349
Betrayed by Love #391
Enamored #420
Reluctant Father #469
Hoodwinked #492
His Girl Friday #528
Hunter #606
Nelson's Brand #618
The Best Is Yet To Come #643
‡The Case of the Mesmerizing
  Boss #702
‡The Case of the Confirmed
  Bachelor #715
‡The Case of the Missing
  Secretary #733
Night of Love #799
Secret Agent Man #829
*That Burke Man #913
Man of Ice #1000
The Patient Nurse #1099

Silhouette Special Edition

Heather's Song #33
The Australian #239
Maggie's Dad #991

For Kathryn Falk and Melinda Helfer
of *Romantic Times*
with love

One

He was very noticeable, and he knew it. He also had a pretty formidable reputation locally with women and he didn't usually turn down blatant invitations. But the wide-eyed scrutiny he was getting from the woman at the corner table only irritated him tonight. The past six months had been difficult, and he'd been drinking too much and womanizing too much...or so his family kept saying. Not that he was listening to them much these days. Not when he knew that they weren't really his family.

She wasn't hard on the eyes. He gave her one encompassing glance that took in everything from the French plait of black hair at her nape, down high, firm breasts under a soft white knit blouse, to a small waist and full hips and long elegant legs in tight jeans. She was sitting at a corner table, a little away from it on one side, with his half brother Dwight, and Dwight's fiancée, Winnie. He didn't know her name, but he was pretty sure that she was Winnie's out-of-town house-guest. Pryor, Wyoming, was a small town, and news traveled fast when anyone had company.

He took another sip of his whiskey and stared at the small shot glass contemplatively. He drank far too much lately. When he started taking women to bed and couldn't remember anything about it the next morning, he needed to take another look at his life, he thought bitterly. Dale Branigan had caught him in a weak moment and now she was hounding him for dates. Not that she was bad-looking, but she reminded him of the excesses that were taking him straight to hell according to Dwight.

He glanced toward Dwight's disapproving face, so unlike his, and deliberately raised the shot glass to his thin lips with a mocking smile. He drained it, but when the bartender asked if he wanted another, he said no. It wasn't Dwight who stopped him. It was the expression on that woman's face who was sitting with Dwight and Winnie. There was something quiet and calming about her face, about the oddly compas-sionate way she was looking at him. What he'd thought was a flirting stare didn't seem to be one. As he met her eyes across the room, he felt a jolt of pure emotion run through him. Odd. He hadn't felt that before. Maybe it was the liquor.

He looked around. The bar was crowded, and there weren't many women around. Thank God Dale wasn't here to pester him. Frequently on a Friday night, he drove up to Billings for a little entertainment. Tonight, he wasn't in the mood. He'd over-heard a chance remark from one of his men and his quick temper had cost him a good mechanic. It was his nature to hit when he was angry. With a soft, cold laugh he considered that he'd probably inherited that trait from his father. From his *real* father, not the man who'd been married to his mother for more than twenty years. Until six months ago, his name had been Gene Nelson and he was accepted by everyone as Hank Nelson's son. But six months ago, Hank Nelson had died—ten years after Gene's mother—and he'd left a will that was as much a confession as a bequeath. It had contained the shocking news that he'd adopted Gene at the age of four.

Gene realized that he was idly sliding the shot glass around on the bar and stopped. He paid for the drink and turned toward the door.

Dwight called to him and he hesitated. His younger half brother was the head honcho at the Triple N Ranch now. That was the biggest blow to his pride. He'd been the eldest son. Now he was the outsider, and Dwight was the rightful heir. That took a lot of getting used to after thirty years.

He cocked his hat over one eye and strode toward Dwight's table, his lean, dark face rigid, his pale green eyes like wet peridots under lashes as thick and black as the straight hair under the gray Stetson.

"You haven't met Gene, have you, Allison?" Winnie asked, smiling. She was blond and petite and very pretty. Her fairness matched Dwight's, who also had blond hair and blue eyes, a fact that had often puzzled Gene. Their sister Marie was equally fair. Only Gene was dark, and he alone had green eyes. His mother had been a blue-eyed blonde, like Hank Nelson. Why had he never connected those stray facts? Perhaps he'd been dodging the issue all along.

"No, we haven't met," Allison said softly. She looked up at Gene with hazel eyes that were his instant undoing. He'd never seen eyes like that. There was something in them that made him feel warm inside. "How do you do, Mr. Nelson?" she asked, and she smiled. It was like sunshine on a cloudy day.

He caught his breath silently. She'd called him Mr. Nelson, but he wasn't a Nelson. He straightened. What the hell, it was the only name he'd ever known. He nodded curtly. "Miss...?"

"Hathoway," she replied.

"Are you on your way back to the ranch?" Dwight asked, his tone reconciliatory, hesitant.

"Yes."

"I'll see you there, then."

Gene let his eyes fall to the woman again, to her gentle oval face. Her eyes and mouth were her best features. She wasn't really pretty, but she had a glow about her. It grew as he looked at her unsmilingly, and he finally realized that she was blushing. Strange response, for a woman her age. She was out of her teens; probably in her mid-twenties.

"Gene, you are coming to the barbecue tomorrow night?" Winnie asked.

He was still staring at Allison. "Maybe." His head moved a little to the side as he looked down at Allison. "Are you Winnie's houseguest?" he asked her, his voice slow and deep, without a noticeable accent.

"Yes," she said. "Just for a couple of weeks, I mean," she stammered. He made her nervous. She'd never felt such an instant attraction to anyone.

Unbeknownst to her, neither had Gene. He was having a hard time trying to drag himself away. This woman made him feel as if he'd suddenly come out of a daze, and he didn't understand why. "I've got to get home," he said, forcing the words out. He nodded curtly and left them, his booted feet heavy on the wood floor, his back arrow-straight.

Allison Hathoway watched him go. She'd never seen anyone quite as fascinating as the departing Mr. Nelson. He looked like a TV cowboy she'd seen once, tall and lean and lithe, with wide shoulders and narrow hips and long, powerful legs. She, who had little if anything to do with men, was so affected by him that she was still flushed and shaking inside from the brief encounter.

"I didn't think he was going to stop," Dwight said with a rueful smile. "He avoids me a lot these days. Marie, too. Except to start fights."

"It isn't getting any easier at home, is it?" Winnie asked her fiancé, laying a small hand on his.

Dwight shook his head as he curled his fingers around hers. "Gene won't talk about it. He just goes on as if nothing has happened. Marie's at the end of her rope, and so am I. We love him, but he's convinced himself that he's no longer part of our family."

Allison listened without understanding what they were talking about.

"Is he much older than you, Dwight?" she asked.

He lifted an eyebrow, smiling at her interest. "About six years. He's thirty-four."

"But he's not a man to risk your heart on," Winnie said softly. "Gene's just gone through a bad time. He's hurt and he's ready to lash out at anybody who gets too close."

"I hate to agree, but she's right," Dwight replied quietly. "Gene's gone from bad to worse in the past few months. Women, liquor, fights. He threw a punch at our mechanic and fired him this morning."

"The man deserved it," Winnie said quietly. "You know what he called Gene."

"He wouldn't have called Gene anything if my brother hadn't started acting like one of the hands instead of the boss," Dwight said angrily. "He hates the routine of working cattle every day. He had the business head and he was good at organization. I'm not. I was better at working cattle and taking care of the shipping and receiving. The will reversed our duties. Now we're both miserable. I can't handle the men, and Gene won't. The ranch is going to pot because he won't buckle down. He drinks on the weekends and the men's morale is at rock bottom. They're looking for excuses to quit or get fired."

"But...he only had one drink at the bar," Allison said softly, puzzled, because one drink surely wasn't that bad.

Dwight lifted a blond eyebrow. "So he did. He kept glancing at you, and then he put down the glass. I was watching. It seemed to bother him. That's the first time I've known him to stop at one drink."

"He always used to," Winnie recalled. "In fact, he hardly ever touched the stuff."

"He's so damned brittle," Dwight sighed. "He can't bend. God, I feel for him! I can imagine how it would be if I were in his shoes. He's so alone."

"Most people are, really," Allison said, her hazel eyes soft and quiet. "And when they hurt, they do bad things sometimes."

Winnie smiled at her warmly. "You'd find excuses for hardened criminals, wouldn't you?" she asked gently. "I suppose that's why you're so good at what you do."

"At what I *did*," Allison corrected. Her eyes fell worriedly to the table. "I don't know that I'll ever be able to do it again."

"You need time," Winnie replied sympathetically. "That's all, Allie. You just need time."

"Something I have in common with your future brother-in-law, I gather," came the reply. Allison sighed and sipped her ginger ale. "I hope you're right."

But that night, alone in bed, the nightmares came again and she woke, as she always did these days, in a cold sweat, trying not to hear the sound of guns, the sound of screams.

She wrapped her white chenille bathrobe around her worn white gown and made her way to the kitchen. Winnie was already there. Her mother was still in bed. Mrs. Manley was no early bird, even if her daughter was.

Allison's long black hair was around her shoulders

in a wavy tangle, her hazel eyes bloodshot, her face pale. She felt dragged out.

"Bad dreams again, I'll bet," Winnie said gently.

Allison managed a wan smile. She accepted the cup of hot black coffee Winnie handed her as they sat down at the kitchen table. "It's better than it was," she said.

"I'm just glad that you came to us," Winnie replied. She was wearing an expensive pink silk ensemble. The Manleys were much better off financially than the Hathoways had ever been, but Mrs. Manley and Allison's late mother had been best friends. As they grew up, Winnie and Allison became best friends, too.

They'd all lived near Bisbee, Arizona, when the girls were young and in school. Then the Manleys had moved to Pryor, Wyoming, when Mr. Manley took another job with an international mining concern. The Hathoways had been reassigned and Allison had gone with them to Central America.

The last few weeks could have been just a bad memory except that Allison was alone now. She'd called Winnie the minute she'd landed in the States again, and Winnie had flown down to Tucson to pick her up. It had been days before Allison could stop crying. Now, at last, she was beginning to heal. Yesterday was the first time Winnie had been able to coax her out among people. Allison was running from the news media that had followed her to Tucson, and she didn't want any attention drawn to her. She'd successfully covered her tracks, but she didn't know for how long.

"The barbecue is tonight. You have to come," Winnie told Allison. "Don't worry," she added quickly when the taller girl froze. "They're all rodeo people that Dwight's introducing me to. Nobody will bother you."

"Dwight's brother said he might be there," Allison murmured.

Winnie groaned. "For God's sake, don't tempt fate by getting too close to Gene. You've just come through one trauma; you don't need another one."

"I know." Allison cupped her cold hands around her coffee cup and closed her eyes. "I suppose I'm pretty vulnerable right now. It's just the aloneness. I've never been really alone before." She looked up and there was faint panic in her face.

"You'll never be alone as long as the Manleys are alive," Winnie said firmly. She laid a warm hand over Allison's forearm. "We all love you very much."

"Yes, I know. Do you know how much I care for all of you, and how grateful I am for a place to stay?" Allison replied sincerely. "I couldn't even go back to the house in Bisbee. Mom and Dad rented it out... Well, before we went to Central America." She faltered. "I was afraid to go near it even for possessions, in case somebody from the press was watching."

"All the furor will die down once the fighting stops," Winnie assured her. "You're being hunted because you have firsthand information about what really happened there. With the occupation forces in control, not much word is getting out. Once the government is well in power, it will become old news and they'll leave you alone. In the meantime, you can stay with us as long as you like.''

"I'm in the way. Your marriage..."

"My marriage isn't for six months," Winnie reminded her with a warm smile. "You'll be my maid of honor. By then, all this will just be a sad memory. You'll have started to live again."

"I hope so," Allison replied huskily. "Oh, I hope so!"

Back at the Nelson place, Gene had just gone into the house to find his half sister, Marie, glaring at him from the living room. She looked like Dwight, except that she was petite and sharp-tongued.

"Dale's been calling again," she said irritably. "She seems to have the idea that she's engaged to you."

"I don't marry one-night stands," he said with deliberate cruelty.

"Then you should make that clear at the beginning," she returned.

His broad shoulders rose and fell. "I was too drunk."

Marie got up and went to him, her expression concerned. "Look at what you're doing to yourself," she said miserably. "This is your home. Dwight and I don't think of you as an outsider, Gene."

"Don't start," he said curtly, his pale green eyes flashing at her.

She threw up her hands with an angry sigh. "You won't listen! You drink, you carouse, you won't even pay attention to the lax discipline that's letting the men goof off half the time. I saw Rance with a bottle in broad daylight the other day!"

"If I see him, I'll do something about him," he said, striding toward the staircase.

"And when will that be? You're too busy having a good time to notice!"

He didn't answer her and he didn't look back. He went upstairs, his booted feet making soft thuds on the carpet.

"What about Dale? What do I tell her if she calls again?" she called after him.

"Tell her I joined a monastery and took vows of chastity," he drawled.

She chuckled. "That'll be the day," she murmured as she went back into the living room. At least he had been sober when he got home last night, she thought. And then she frowned. Not his usual style on a Friday night, she pondered.

It wasn't until later in the morning, when Dwight told her about his meeting with Allison, that his behavior registered.

"You mean, he looked at her and put the shot glass down?" Marie asked, all eyes.

"He certainly did," Dwight replied. Gene had gone out to check on the branding. Considering the size of the ranch and the number of new calves, it was much more than a couple of days' work. "He couldn't seem to keep his eyes off her."

"Is she pretty?" Marie asked.

He shook his head. "Nice. Very sweet. And a passable figure. But no, she's no beauty. Odd, isn't it, for Gene to even notice a woman like that? His tastes run to those brassy, experienced women he meets at rodeos. But Allison seemed to captivate him.''

"If she influenced him enough to keep him sober on a Friday night, I take my hat off to her," Marie said with genuine feeling. "He was like his old self last night. It was nice, seeing him that way. He's been so different for the past few months."

"Yes. I know it's hurt him. I never realized how much until I saw him coming apart in front of my eyes. Knowing about his real father has driven him half-mad.''

"We can't help who our parents are," Marie said. "And Gene wouldn't be like that man in a million years. Surely he knows it?''

"He mumbled something about never having kids of his own because of his bad blood, one night when he was drinking," Dwight confided. He sighed and finished his coffee. "I wish we could find some way to cope with it. He has no peace.''

Marie fingered her coffee cup thoughtfully. "Maybe he can find it with our Miss Hathoway," she mused, her eyes twinkling as they met his. "If she had that effect from a distance, imagine what it could be like at close range?''

"Except that she isn't Gene's kind of woman," he replied, and began to tell her all about the quiet Miss Hathoway.

Marie whistled. "My gosh. Poor kid.''

"She's an amazing lady," he said, smiling. "Winnie's very fond of her. So fond that she'll discourage her from even looking at Gene, much less anything else.''

"I can see why. The angel and the outlaw," she murmured, and smiled gently. "I guess I was daydreaming."

"Nothing wrong with dreams," he told her as he got up from the table. "But they won't run a ranch."

"Or organize a barbecue," Marie said, smiling. "Good luck with the books."

He groaned. "I'll have us in the poor house in another few months. If Gene was more approachable, I'd ask him to switch duties with me."

"Could you do that?"

"No reason why not," he said. "But he hasn't been in a listening mood."

"Don't give up. There's always tomorrow."

He laughed. "Tell him." He left her sitting there, still looking thoughtful.

Two

"Are you sure this looks all right on me?" Allison asked worriedly as she stared into the mirror at the low neckline of the strapless sundress Winnie had loaned her for the barbecue. They'd spent a lazy day at home, and now it was almost time to leave for the Nelsons' Triple N Ranch.

"Will you stop fussing? You look fine," Winnie assured her. "You've been out of touch with fashion for a while. Don't worry, it's perfectly proper. Even for Pryor, Wyoming," she added with a mischievous grin.

Allison sighed at her reflection in the full-length mirror. The young woman staring back at her looked like a stranger. Her long, dark hair was loose and wavy, framing her lovely oval face to its best advantage. She'd used mascara to emphasize her hazel eyes and she'd applied foundation and lipstick much more liberally than usual. Too, the off-the-shoulder sundress with its elasticized bodice certainly did make her appear sophisticated. Its daring green, white and black pattern was exotic and somehow suited her tall, full-figured body. The strappy white sandals Winnie had loaned her completed the outfit.

Winnie modeled dresses for a local department store, so she was able to buy clothes at a considerable discount. She knew all sorts of beauty secrets, ways of making the most of her assets and downplaying the minor flaws of face and figure. She'd used them to advantage on her houseguest. Allison hardly recognized herself.

"I always knew you'd be a knockout if you were dressed and made up properly." Winnie nodded, approving her handiwork. "I'm glad you finally gave in and let me do my thing. You'll have the bachelors flitting around you like bees around clover. Dwight has a friend who'd be perfect for you, if he just shows up. He'll be bowled over."

"That'll be the day." Allison laughed softly, but she was secretly hoping that one particular bachelor named Gene might give her at least a second glance. She didn't know what kind of problems he had, but knowing that he'd been hurt, too, gave her a fellow feeling for him. It wasn't good to be alone when you were in pain.

"You're a late bloomer. Trust me." Winnie dragged her out of the bedroom and down the hall to the living room, where her mother was waiting. "Mom, look what I did to Allie," she called.

Mrs. Manley, a tall, graying woman, smiled as she turned to greet the two young women. "My, what a change," she said. "You look lovely, Allie. I wish your parents could see you."

Allie sobered. "Yes. So do I, Mrs. Manley."

"Forgive me," the older woman said. "Your mother and I were best friends for thirty years. But as hard as it is for me, I know it must be ten times harder for you."

"Life goes on," Allie said. She sighed, spreading her long, elegant fingers over the full skirt of the dress. "Isn't this a dream? I don't know how to thank you and Winnie for letting me stay with you. I really had nowhere else to go."

"I'm sure you have plenty of friends besides us, even if they are spread around the world a bit," Winnie chided. She hugged Allison. "But I'm still your best one. Remember when we were in seventh grade together back in Bisbee and we had to climb the mountain every day after school to get to our houses?"

"I miss Arizona sometimes," Allison said absently.

"I don't," Mrs. Manley said, shaking her head. "I used to have nightmares about falling into the Lavender Pit." She shuddered delicately. "It suited me when Winnie's father changed jobs and we moved here. Of course, if I'd known he was going to have to travel all over the world, I might have had second thoughts. He's gone almost all the time lately."

"He'll retire next year," Winnie reminded her.

"Yes, so he will." Mrs. Manley smiled and

changed the subject. "You two had better get going, or you'll be late. The barbecue's at the Nelsons'?"

"Yes. Dwight invited us." Winnie grinned. "I'll have to make sure he doesn't toss me into the corral with those wild horses and ride off with Allie."

"Small chance when you're engaged." Allison grinned.

Winnie drove them to the Nelson place in her small Japanese car, a sporty model that suited her. Allison could drive, but she didn't have a current license. Where she'd been for the past two years, she hadn't needed one.

"Before we get there," Winnie said with a worried glance at Allison, "remember what I said and don't get too close to Gene. I don't think he'd let you get near him anyway—he's pretty standoffish around shy little innocents. But I wasn't kidding when I told you he was a dangerous customer. Even his brother and sister walk wide around him lately."

"He can't be that bad," Allison said gently and smiled.

"Don't you believe it." Winnie wasn't convinced. She scowled. "You watch yourself."

"All right. I will," she promised, but she had her fingers crossed beside her. "Is he by chance a jilted man, embittered by the faithlessness of some jaded woman, or was he treated horribly by his mother?" she added dryly.

"Gene doesn't get jilted by women, and his mother was a saint, according to Dwight," Winnie recalled. "A really wonderful woman who was loved by the whole community. She died about ten years ago. His father was a small-time rancher with a big heart. They were happily married. His...father died about six months ago."

Allison wondered at the hesitation in Winnie's voice when she talked about the late Mr. Nelson. "Do you know what's wrong with Gene, then?" she persisted.

"Yes. But I can't tell you," was the quiet reply. "It's not really any of my business, and Dwight's already been asked too many questions by the whole community. I don't mean to sound rude, and I trust you with my life," Winnie added, "but it's Gene's business."

"I understand."

"No, you don't, but Dwight may tell you one day. Or Marie."

"Is Marie like Gene or Dwight?"

"In coloring, she's like Dwight, blond and blue-eyed. Gene's...different. More hardheaded. Fiery."

"I gathered that. Doesn't he ever smile?"

"Sometimes," Winnie said. "Usually when he's about to hit somebody. He isn't an easygoing man. He's arrogant and proud and just a little too quick on the trigger to be good company. You'll find all that out. I just don't want you to find it out at close range, the hard way."

"I can take care of myself, you know," Allison mused. "I've been doing it in some pretty rough places for a long time."

"I know. But there's a big difference in what you've been doing and a man-woman relationship." She glanced at Allison as she turned into a long, graveled driveway. "Honestly, for a twenty-five-year-old woman, you're just hopelessly backward, and I mean that in the nicest possible way. It isn't as if you've had the opportunity to lead a wild life. But you've been criminally exposed in some ways and criminally sheltered in others. I don't think your parents ever really considered you when they made their plans."

Allison laughed gently. "Yes, they did. I'm just like them, Winnie. I loved every minute of what we all did together, and I'll miss it terribly, even now." Her eyes clouded. "Things happen as God means them to. I can cope."

"It was such a waste, though...."

"On, no," Allison said, remembering the glowing faces she'd seen, the purpose and peace in the dark eyes. "No, it was never a waste. They're still alive, in the work they did, in the lives they changed."

"I won't argue with you," Winnie said gently. "We've kept in touch and remained friends all these long years since we were in school together in Bisbee. You're still the sister I never had. You'll have a home as long as I'm alive."

Tears sprang to Allison's big eyes. She hurriedly dashed them away. "If the circumstances were reversed, I hope you know that I'd do the same thing for you."

"I know," Winnie said. She wiped away a tear of her own.

There was a crowd of cars in the front driveway at the Nelsons' after they'd wound their way up past the towering lodgepole pines and aspen trees to the big stone house, backed by jagged high mountains.

"Isn't it just heaven?" Allison sighed involuntarily. "Wyoming is beautiful."

"Yes, it certainly is. I can happily spend the rest of my life here. Now, Allie, you aren't planning to sit behind bushes all night, are you?" she muttered. "The whole idea of this party is to meet people."

"For *you* to meet people," Allison emphasized. "You're the one who's getting married, not me."

"You can take advantage of it, all the same. These are interesting people, too. Most of them are rodeo folks, and the rest are cattlemen or horse breeders."

"You're making me nervous," Allison said, fidgeting in her seat as Winnie parked the car behind a silver-gray Lincoln. "I don't know anything about rodeo or horses or cattle."

"No time like the present to learn," Winnie said easily. "Come on. Out of there."

"Is this trip really necessary?" Allison murmured, swinging her long, elegant legs out of the car. "I could stay in the car and make sure it doesn't roll down the hill."

"Not a chance, my friend. After all the work I've put in on you today, I want to show you off."

"Gloating over your artistry, I gather?" Allison primped. "Well, let's spread me among the peasants, then."

"I'd forgotten your Auntie Mame impersonation," Winnie winced. "Don't lay it on too thick, now."

"Cross my heart and hope to die," Allison agreed. She drew an imaginary line across her stomach.

"Your heart isn't down there," Winnie said worriedly.

"Yes, it is. The only thing I really love is food, so that's where my heart is. Right?"

"I give up."

Allison followed her friend up the wide stone steps to where Dwight Nelson waited on the porch, his blond hair gleaming in the fading sunlight.

"There you are!" he chuckled, and swung a beaming Winnie up in his arms to kiss her soundly. "Hello, Allie, glad you could come," he told the other woman and suddenly stopped, his eyes widening as he stared at her. "Allie? That is you, isn't it?"

Allison sent a dry look in her friend's direction. "Go ahead. Gloat," she dared.

"I did it all," Winnie said, smiling haughtily. "Just look. Isn't she a dish?"

"Indeed she is, and if I hadn't seen you first..." Dwight began.

Winnie stomped on his big foot through his boot. "Hold it right there, buster, before you talk yourself into a broken leg. You're all mine, and don't you forget it."

"As if I could." Dwight winced, flexing his booted foot. "You look gorgeous, Allie, now will you tell her I was kidding?"

"He was kidding," Allie told Winnie.

"All right. You're safe, this time." Winnie slid her arm around Dwight's lean waist. "Where's Marie?"

"Around back," he said, grimacing as he glanced toward the sound of a local band beyond the arch in the surrounding wall. "Gene's out there."

"Gene and Marie don't get along," Winnie told Allison.

"That's like saying old-time cowboys and old-time
Indians don't get along." Dwight sighed. "Fortunately the guests will keep them from killing each
other in public. Mother used to spend her life sepa-
rating them. It was fine while Gene was abroad for a
year on a selling trip. We actually had peaceful meals.
Now we have indigestion and a new cook every
month." He pursed his lips. "Speaking of food, let's
go see if there's any left." Dwight glanced over their
heads toward the driveway. "I think you two are the
last people we expected."

"The best always are, darling," Winnie said, smiling up at him with sparkling affection.

Allison had to fight her inclination to be jealous,
but if anyone ever deserved happiness, Winnie did.
She had a heart as big as the whole world.

She followed the engaged couple through the stone
arch to the tents that had been set up with tables and
chairs positioned underneath it to seat guests. A huge
steer carcass was roasting over an open fire while an
Oriental man basted it with sauce, smiling and nodding as two women, one of whom Winnie whispered
was Marie Nelson, carried off platters of it to the
tables.

Other pots contained baked beans and Brunswick
stew, which were being served as well, along with
what had to be homemade rolls.

"It smells heavenly," Allison sighed, closing her
eyes to inhale the sweet aroma.

"It tastes heavenly, too," Dwight said. "I grabbed
a sample on my way around the house. Here, sit down
and dig in."

He herded them toward the first tent, where there were several vacant seats, but he and Winnie were waylaid by a couple they knew and Allison was left to make her own way to the long table.

She took a plate and utensils from the end of the table, along with a glass of ice tea, and sat down. Platters of barbecue and rolls, and bowls of baked beans and Brunswick stew, were strategically placed all along the table. Allison filled her plate with small portions. It had been a long time since she'd felt comfortable eating her fill, and she had difficulty now with the sheer volume of food facing her.

Gene Nelson was standing nearby talking to a visiting cattleman when he saw Allison sit down alone at the table. His eyes had found her instantly, as if he'd known the second she'd arrived. He didn't understand his fierce attraction to her, even if she did look good enough to eat tonight. Her dress was blatantly sexy, and she seemed much more sophisticated than she had in the bar with Dwight and Winnie. Winnie was a model, and he knew she had some liberated friends. He'd even dated Winnie once, which was why Dwight's fiancée had such a bad opinion of him. Not that he'd gotten very far. Dwight had cut him out about the second date, and women were so thick on the ground that he'd never given Dwight's appropriation of his date a second thought. That might have added to Winnie's disapproval, he mused, the fact that he hadn't wanted her enough to fight for her. It was nothing personal. He'd simply never wanted any woman enough to fight for her. They were all alike. Well, most all alike, he thought, staring helplessly at

Allison, with her long, dark hair almost down to her narrow waist.

He sighed heavily as he watched her. It had been a while since he'd had a woman. His body ached for sensual oblivion, for something to ease the emotional pain he'd been through. Not that he remembered much about that supposedly wild night with Dale Branigan that had kept her hounding him. In fact, he hardly remembered it at all. Maybe that was why his body ached so when he looked at Allison. These dry spells were hell on the nerves.

Allison felt his gaze and lifted her hazel eyes to seek his across the space that separated them. Oh, but he was handsome, she thought dizzily. He was dressed in designer jeans and a neat white burgundy patterned Western shirt with pearl snaps instead of buttons. He wore a burgundy bandanna around his neck and hand-tooled leather boots. His head was bare, his hair almost black and faintly damp, as if he'd just come from a shower. He was more masculine and threatening than any man Allison had ever known, and the way he looked at her made her tingle all over.

She shouldn't encourage him; she knew she shouldn't. But she couldn't stop looking at him. Her life had been barren of eligible men. It was inevitable that she might be attracted to the first nice-looking bachelor she met, she told herself.

If that look in her eyes wasn't an invitation, he was blind, Gene thought, giving in to it with hardly a struggle. He threw down the cigarette he was smoking and ground it out under his heel. He excused himself, leaving the cattleman with another associate, and picked up a glass of beer and a plate and utensils before he joined Allison. He threw a long leg over the wooden bench at the table and sat down, glancing at the tiny portions on her plate.

"Don't you like barbecue?" he asked coolly, and he didn't smile.

She looked up into pale green eyes in a lean face with a deeply tanned complexion. Her eyes were a nice medium hazel flecked with green and gold, but his were like peridot—as pale as green ice under thick black lashes. His black hair was straight and conventionally cut, parted on the left side and pulled back from a broad forehead. He had high cheekbones and a square chin with a hint of a cleft in it. His mouth was as perfectly formed as the mouth on a Greek statue—wide and firm and faintly chiseled, with a thin upper lip and an only slightly fuller lower one. He wasn't smiling, and he studied Allison with a blatantly familiar kind of scrutiny. It wasn't the first time a man had undressed her with his eyes, but it was the first time it had affected her so completely. She wanted to pull the tablecloth off the table and wrap herself in it.

But that wouldn't do, she told herself. Hadn't she learned that the only way to confront a predator was with steady courage? Her sense of humor came to her rescue, and she warmed to the part she was playing.

"I said, don't you like barbecue?" he repeated. His voice was like velvet, and very deep. The kind of voice that would sound best, she imagined, in intimacy. She started at her own thoughts. She must be in need of rest, to be thinking such things about a total stranger, even if he was lithe and lean and attractive.

"Oh, I like barbecue," she answered with a demure smile. "I'm just not used to having it cut off the cow in front of me."

He smiled faintly, a quirk of his mouth that matched the arrogant set of his head. "Do tell."

"Do tell what?" she asked with what she hoped was a provocative glance from under the thick lashes that mascara had lengthened.

He was a little disappointed at her easy flirting. He'd rather expected her to be shy and maidenly. But it certainly wouldn't be the first time he'd been mistaken about a woman. He lifted a thick eyebrow. "Give me time. I'll think up something."

"A reason to stay alive," she sighed, touching a hand to her chest. "I do hope you aren't married with six children, Mr. Nelson. I would hate to spoil the barbecue by throwing myself off the roof."

His eyes registered mild humor. "I'm not married."

"You must wear a disguise in public," she mused.

He studied her with pursed lips for a minute before he picked up his plate and glass and came around the table. Her heart skipped when he sat down beside her—very close. He smelled of soap and cologne, potent to a woman who wasn't used to civilized men in any form.

"You didn't come alone, I suppose," he mused, watching her closely. "Let me get a few bites of this under my belt so that I'll have enough strength to beat your escort to his knees."

"Oh, I don't have one of those," she assured him, hiding her nervousness in humor, as she always had. "I came with Winnie."

"That spares my knuckles." He was flirting, too, but she appealed to him.

"Have you known Winnie a long time?" he asked pleasantly.

"Yes," she said. "We've been friends since we were kids, back in Arizona."

Winnie had never mentioned her, but then, he hadn't been around Winnie that much since she'd become engaged to Dwight. And these days, he had very little to say to Dwight.

"You said at the bar that you'd only be here a couple of weeks. How long have you been in Pryor?"

She smiled faintly. "Just a few days. I'm looking forward to a nice visit with Winnie. It's been years since we spent any time together." She couldn't very well tell him that the length of her stay depended on whether or not she could keep anybody in Pryor from knowing who she was and why she was here. She'd successfully ducked the media since her arrival. She didn't want them after her again.

"Have you done much sightseeing?" he asked, letting his eyes fall to her bare shoulders with bold interest.

"Not yet. But I'm enjoying myself. It's nice to have a vacation from work."

That sounded odd, as if she'd forced the words out and didn't mean them. One pale eye narrowed even more. His gaze slid over her curiously, lingering on the thrust of her breasts under the low neckline.

"What do you normally do—when you aren't visiting old friends?" he asked.

"I'm a vamp," she murmured dryly, enjoying herself as she registered his mild surprise. It was like being an actress, playing a part. It took her mind off the horror of the past months.

"No, I won't buy that," he said after a minute. "What do you really do?" he persisted, fingering his glass.

She lifted her own glass to her lips, to give her time to think. He didn't look stupid. She couldn't say anything that might give her away to Winnie's neighbors, especially her future brother-in-law.

"I'm in the salvage business," she said finally.

He stared at her.

She laughed. "Oh, no, I didn't mean used cars and scrap metal and such. I'm in the human salvage business. I'm…" she hesitated, searching for something that wouldn't be a total lie.

"You're what?" he asked.

He was dangerously inquisitive, and almost too quick for her. She had to throw him off the track before he tripped her up and got at the truth. She lifted her eyebrows. "Are you by any chance the reincarnation of the Spanish Inquisition?"

"I don't even speak Spanish," he said. He smiled slowly, interested despite his suspicions. "How old are you?"

"Sir, you take my breath away!" she exclaimed.

His eyes fell to her mouth. "Is that a request?" he murmured, and there was suddenly a world of experience in the pale eyes that skimmed her mouth, in the deepness of his soft voice.

Her hand trembled as she put down the glass. He was out of her league and she was getting nervous. It didn't take a college degree to understand what he meant. "You're going too fast," she blurted out.

He leaned back, studying her through narrow eyes. She was a puzzle, a little mass of contradictions. But in spite of that, she appealed to him as no one else had in recent years.

"Okay, honey," he said after a minute, and smiled faintly. "I'll put on the brakes." He took another bite of barbecue and washed it down with what looked and smelled like beer.

"How old are you?" she asked without meaning to, her eyes on the hard lines of his face. She imagined that he had a poker face when he wanted to, that he could hide what he was feeling with ease. She knew his age, because Dwight had told her, but it wouldn't do to let him know that she'd been asking questions about him from the very first time she saw him.

He glanced at her, searching her wide, curious eyes. "I'm thirty-four."

She dropped her eyes to his chin and further down, to his broad chest.

"Too old for you, cupcake?" he asked carelessly.

"I'm twenty-five," she said.

His dark brows drew together. He'd thought she was younger than that. Yes, she had a few lines in her face, and even a thread or two of gray in her dark hair. Nine years his junior. Not much difference in

years, and at her age, she couldn't possibly be innocent. His heart accelerated as he studied what he
could see of her body in the revealing dress and wondered what she'd look like without it. She was nicely
shaped, and if that beautiful bow of a mouth was anything to go by, she was probably going to be a delicious little morsel. If only she wasn't best friends with
Winnie.

He studied her again. She really was a puzzle.
Young, and then, suddenly, not young. There had
been a fleeting expression in her eyes when he'd
asked her about her profession—an expression that
confused him. He had a feeling that she wasn't at all
what she seemed. But, like him, she seemed to hide
her emotions.

"Twenty-five. You're no baby, are you?" he murmured.

Her eyes came up and that expression was in them
again, before she erased it and smiled. Fascinating, he
thought, like watching an actress put on her stage
makeup.

"No. I'm no baby," she agreed softly, her mind
on the ordeal she'd been through and not really on
the question. She didn't realize what she was saying
to him with her words, that she was admitting to experience that she didn't have.

He felt his body reacting to the look in her eyes
and he stiffened with surprise. It usually took longer
for a woman to affect him so physically. He wouldn't
let her look away. The electricity began to flow between them and his eyes narrowed as he saw her
mouth part helplessly. She was close, and she smelled

of floral cologne that drifted up, mingling with the spicy scent of barbecue and the malt smell of his beer.

His gaze dropped to the cleft between her breasts and lingered there, on skin as smooth and pink as a sun-ripened peach. His chest rose and fell roughly as he tried to imagine how her breasts would feel under his open mouth...

The sudden shock of voices made the glass of beer jerk in his lean hand.

"Did you think we'd deserted you?" Dwight asked Allison, echoing Winnie's greeting. "I see you've found Gene," he added, patting the older man on the shoulder as he paused beside him. "Be careful that he doesn't try to drag you under the table."

"Watch it," the older man returned humorously. But his eyes were glinting, and he knew that Dwight wouldn't mistake the warning even if it flew right past his new acquaintance.

Dwight understood, all right, but he didn't do the expected thing and go away.

"You don't mind if we join you, do you?"

"Of course not," Allison said, frowning slightly at Gene's antagonism. She glanced from him to Dwight. "You two don't favor each other a lot."

There was an embarrassed silence and Winnie actually grimaced.

"No, we don't, do we?" Gene's eyes narrowed as they glanced off Dwight's apologetic ones. "We all share the same mother, but not the same father." He leaned back and laughed coldly. "Isn't that right, Dwight?"

Dwight went red. "Allison didn't know," he said

curtly. "You're always on the defensive lately, Gene."

The past few months came back to torment him. He stared at his half brother with eyes as cold and unfeeling as green stone. "I can't forget. Why should you be expected to?"

"You're family," Dwight said, almost apologetically. "Or you would be if you'd stop lashing out at everybody. You're always giving Marie hell."

"She gives it back." Gene swallowed his drink and put the glass on the table. His eyes went to a silent, curious Allison. "You don't understand, do you, cupcake?" he asked with a smile that was mocking and cruel. "I had a different father than Dwight and Marie. I was adopted. Something my mother and stepfather apparently didn't think I needed to know until my stepfather died six months ago."

She watched him get up, and her eyes were soft and compassionate as they searched his. "I'm sorry," she said gently. "It must have been very hard to find it out so suddenly."

He hated that softness in her eyes, that warmth. He didn't want compassion from her. The only thing he might ever want from her was that silky body, but this was hardly the time to be thinking about it. He glared at her. "I don't want pity, thanks."

"Gene, for God's sake," Dwight ground out.

"Don't worry. I won't spoil your party." He caught a strand of Allison's dark hair and tugged it. "Stay away from me. I'm bad medicine. Ask anybody."

He walked away without another word, lighting a cigarette as he went.

Allison's eyes followed him, and she almost felt his pain. Poor, tormented man....

"Don't make the mistake of feeling sorry for him," Dwight told her when Gene was out of earshot. "Pity is the last thing he wants or needs. He has to come to grips with it himself."

"Where is his real father?" Allison asked quietly.

He started to speak, but before he could, a smaller, female version of Dwight slammed down into a chair beside Winnie.

"So he's gone," Marie Nelson muttered. "Dwight, he's just impossible. I can't even talk to him...." She colored, looking at Allison. "Sorry," she said. "You must be Allison. Winnie's been hiding you for days, I thought she'd never introduce us!" she said with a smile. "I didn't mean to start airing the family linen in public. You'll have to excuse me. Gene always sets me off."

"What's he done now?" Dwight groaned.

"He seduced my best friend," she muttered.

"Dale Branigan is not your best friend," Dwight reminded her. "She's a divorcée with claws two inches long, and if anybody got seduced it was Gene, not her. It's not his fault that she won't realize it was a one-shot fling for him."

"I don't mean Dale," she sighed. "I meant Jessie."

"Gene's never been near Jessie," Dwight said shortly.

"She says he has. She says—"

"Marie," he said, calling her by name for the first time and confirming Allison's suspicions, "Jessie couldn't tell the truth if her life depended on it. She's been crazy about Gene for years and it's gotten her nowhere. This is just a last-ditch effort to get him to marry her. I'm telling you, it won't work. She can't blackmail him to the altar."

"She might not be lying," Marie said, although not with as much conviction as before. "You know how Gene is with women."

"I don't think you do," Dwight said. "Jessie isn't even his type. He likes sophisticated, worldly women."

Marie leaned back in her chair with a sigh. "Poor Jessie."

"Poor Jessie," Dwight agreed. "Now say hello to Winnie."

"Hi, Winnie," Marie greeted belatedly, and smiled. "It's nice to see you again. And I'm glad Allison could come," she added, smiling. She didn't add what Dwight had said about the effect she had on Gene. Now that she'd seen it for herself, she was intrigued. There was indeed something very special about Miss Hathoway, and apparently Gene had noticed it.

"Thank you for inviting me," Allison replied sincerely. "I wouldn't want to impose."

"You aren't. How do you like Wyoming?"

"Very much. It's beautiful."

"We think so." Marie studied her curiously. "Winnie's very secretive about you. You aren't a fugitive Hell's Angel or anything, are you?" she teased, trying not to give away what Dwight had told her about the other woman.

"I don't think so," Allison said, leaning forward to add, "but what if I have memory failure and I've got a motorcycle stashed somewhere?"

"As long as it's a Harley-Davidson, it's okay." Marie grinned. "I've always wanted to ride one."

"Horses, okay. Motorcycles, never." Her brother grinned. "She's a former rodeo champion, or did I mention it?" he added.

"Are you, really?" Allison asked, all eyes.

"Gene, too," Marie said, sighing. "He was world champion roper one year, before he hurt his hand. He doesn't compete anymore. He's bitter about so many things. I wish he could stop blaming Dwight and me. We love him, you know. But he won't believe any of us do."

"Maybe he'll come around someday. It's a blessing that he has so much to do that he doesn't have time to brood," Dwight added. "We supply broncs and bulls for rodeos," he told Allison. "It's a full-time job, especially since we're always shipping or receiving livestock. The paperwork alone is a nightmare, even with the computers."

"It sounds complicated. And dangerous," she added, thinking about the wildness of the animals involved. She wasn't a rodeo fan, but she'd seen the kind of animals cowboys had to ride in competition when she and Winnie had lived in Arizona.

"Working around livestock is always dangerous," Dwight agreed. "But it goes with the territory."

"And we have a good safety record," Marie

chimed in. "Have you ever seen a real rodeo, Allison?"

"Yes," Allison nodded. "Once, when Winnie and I were little."

"I remember the candy better than I remember the rodeo," Winnie laughed. "I imagine Allie does, too."

"I'm afraid you're right," Allison agreed.

"We'll make a fan of you, if you stay here long enough," Dwight promised. "How about some music, Marie? We might as well drag the band out of the barbecue and make them work."

"I'll get them started."

The dancing was fun, but by the time Allison and Winnie went home, Gene Nelson hadn't made another appearance and Allison was disappointed. She was fascinated by him, despite what she'd heard about his reputation. He liked sophisticated women, and tonight she'd pretended to be one. But he'd walked away and left her. She sighed miserably. Even when she was pretending to be a siren, she was still just plain old Allison, she thought dully. It was too much to hope for, that a man like Gene would give her a second glance.

With determination, she smiled and danced and socialized. But her heart wasn't in it. Without the elusive Mr. Nelson, everything had gone flat.

The elusive Mr. Nelson was, in fact, feeling the same way. He'd had to force himself to leave the barbecue, because he'd wanted to dance with Allison. But getting involved with her would only create more problems and he'd had enough. He thought about going into town to the bar, but that felt flat, too. He was losing his taste for liquor and wild women. Maybe he'd caught a virus or something.

He strolled past the bunkhouse, hearing loud laughter, led by the redheaded Rance. It was Saturday night, and he couldn't forbid the men liquor on their own time. But one of these days, he was going to have to confront that venomous rider. He'd been needling Gene for days. The man was sweet on Dale Branigan, and fiercely jealous of Gene. He could have told him there was no need, but it wouldn't have done any good.

He kept walking, his mind still on the way Allison had looked in that sundress. He paused to check two of the sick calves in the barn, marveling at how much he'd changed in just one day and one night. Maybe it was his age, he thought. Then a picture of Allison Hathoway's soft hazel eyes burned into his brain and he groaned. With a muttered curse, he saddled a horse and went out to check on the night herders—something he hadn't done in months.

Three

Allison wasn't comfortable talking to Winnie about Gene Nelson, but she was too curious about him not to ask questions. He'd warned her away himself, telling her that he was bad medicine. But she was attracted despite the warnings. Secretly she wondered if it could be because of them. She'd led a conventional life all the way, never putting a step wrong. A renegade was bound to appeal to her.

"You can't get involved with him," Winnie said quietly when Allison couldn't resist questioning her the next day.

"He didn't seem like a bad man," Allison protested.

"I didn't say he was," Winnie replied, and her expression was sympathetic. "In fact, there isn't a nicer man than Gene. But he's gone wild since he found out about his father. You heard what Marie accused him of yesterday. She wasn't kidding. Gene makes no secret that he has only one use for a woman, and he's done a lot of hard drinking and hard living in the past few months. Because everybody around Pryor knows it, just being seen with him could ruin your reputation. That's why I don't want you to go out with him. I'd never begrudge you a little happiness, but Gene could cost you your respectability. And that's something you can't afford to lose, my friend, in your chosen vocation.''

"Yes, I know,'' Allison murmured. Her heart sank. Winnie was drowning all her dreams. "You said that Gene didn't know about his real father?''

"No. He was just four when his mother divorced his father and married Hank Nelson,'' Winnie said, startling her. "Until six months ago, when his stepfather died, he never knew that he wasn't a blood Nelson.''

Allison's tender heart ached for him. "Poor man,'' she said huskily. "How terrible, to find out like that!''

"It's been terrible for all of them,'' Winnie said honestly. "Don't get me wrong. Dwight and Marie don't feel any differently now than they ever did about Gene, but it's changed everything for him. He worshiped Hank.''

"No wonder he's embittered,'' Allison said softly.

"None of that,'' Winnie murmured dryly. "Your soft heart will be your undoing yet. Now let's talk about something besides Gene. I don't think he's got a soft spot anymore, but he could hurt you if you tried to find it, even for the best of reasons.''

"Yes, I know," Allison replied. "I sensed that, too. But you don't need to worry," she added with a sad smile. "I'm not the type of woman who could appeal to a man like him. He's very handsome and suave. I'm just...me."

"You weren't yourself at the barbecue," her friend murmured tongue in cheek. "You were Auntie Mame and Holly Golightly tied up with a red ribbon. Gene has no idea who and what you really are, and that kind of secret is dangerous to keep."

"Any kind of secret is dangerous to keep," she replied with a gentle smile.

"Amen. Just trust me and keep your distance." She patted Allison's hand gently. "Don't underestimate your own attractions, my friend. You're dishy when you dress up, and that warm heart of yours attracts everyone, including men like Gene."

"It never has before," Allison sighed. "Well, not the right kind of men, anyway."

"One of these days the right man is going to come along. If anybody deserves him, you do."

Allison smiled. "Thanks. I could return the compliment. I like your Dwight very much."

"So do I."

"Will you live with his family when you marry?"

"No," Winnie returned, grateful for the change of subject. "There's another house on the ranch, where Dwight's grandfather used to live. It's being remodeled, and we'll live there. I'll take you to see it one day, if you like."

"I would."

Winnie smiled. "You're so much better than you

were when you came here,'' she said gently. "Is it easing off a little?''

Allison nodded. "Every day, thanks to you and your mother.''

"That's what we both hoped. Dad will be home soon, and then we can do some sightseeing. You know I'm hopeless at finding things, and mother hates to drive distances. There's a lot of history around here.''

"I know. I read all the books I could find about northern Wyoming before I ever dreamed I might actually come here.'' She lowered her eyes. "I had hoped it would be for a happier reason, though.''

"So did I.'' Winnie sipped coffee. "What do you want to see?''

"The nightly rodeo in Cody,'' came the immediate reply. "Not to mention the Western museum there. And there's a place called Shoshone Canyon just outside it, on the way to Yellowstone…''

"Shoshone Canyon gives me the cold willies,'' Winnie said, shivering. "It's eerie, especially when you have to come across the dam to Cody, through the mountain tunnel. I only have to go that way when we're coming back from Yellowstone National Park, thank God. Cody is northwest of here, so we can avoid the canyon altogether.''

"You chicken, you,'' Allison gasped. "I'd love it!''

"I imagine you would. Well, we'll go when Dad gets back, but I'll wear a blindfold.''

"I'll make sure you have one,'' Allison laughed.

There was no more mention of Gene Nelson, even if he did seem to haunt Allison's dreams.

Then, all at once, she seemed to run into him everywhere. She waved to him in town as he drove by in his big Jeep, and he waved back with a smile. She saw him on his horse occasionally as she drove past the ranch with Winnie, and he seemed to watch for her. When she and Winnie visited Dwight, he sometimes paused in the doorway to talk, and his green eyes ran over her with frank curiosity as he joined in the conversation. It always seemed to be about cattle or horses or rodeo, and Allison never understood it, but then it didn't matter. She just loved looking at Gene.

He noticed that rapt stare of hers and was amused by it. Women had always chased him, but there was something different about this one. She was interested in him, but too shy to flirt or play up to him. Ironically that interested him more than a blatant invitation would have.

He began to look for her after that, despite his misgivings about getting involved. She stirred something inside him that he didn't even know he possessed. It was irritating, but he felt as if he'd been caught in an avalanche, and he couldn't stop it.

A few days after the barbecue he noticed Winnie's car going past the ranch, with a passenger, on the way in to Pryor. And he'd found an excuse to go into town himself. To get a new rope, he said. The ranch had enough ropes to furnish Pancho Villa's army already, but it was an excuse if he really needed one to appease his conscience.

That was how Allison came upon him, seemingly accidentally, in Pryor that afternoon while she was picking up some crocheting thread for Mrs. Manley and Winnie was having a fitting for her wedding gown.

He was coming out of the feed store with what looked like a new rope in one lean hand. He'd been working. He was wearing stained jeans with muddy boots and dusty bat-wing chaps. A worn and battered tan Stetson was cocked over one pale green eye, and he needed another shave, even though it was midafternoon. He looked totally out of sorts.

In fact, he was, and Allison was the reason for his bad humor. All the reasons why he should snub her came falling into his brain. It didn't do any good, of course, to tell himself that she was the last complication he needed right now. Miss Chic Society there wasn't cut out for ranch life or anything more than a wild fling, and he was beginning to feel his age. Instead of running around with wild women, he needed to be thinking about a wife and kids. Except that kids might be out of the question, considering the character of his real father. His expression hardened. Besides that, considering his reputation with women, it was going to be hard to find a decent woman who'd be willing to marry him. This wouldn't be a bad time to work on improving his image, and he couldn't do that by linking himself with another sophisticated party girl. Which Miss Hathaway seemed to be, given her performance at the barbecue.

Of course, it wasn't that easy to put the brakes on his interest. Now here she stood, looking at him with those big hazel eyes and making his body ache. And he'd initiated the confrontation.

"Hello, Mr. Nelson," she said, smiling at him. "Out looking for a lost cow?" she added, nodding toward the rope in his hand.

His eyebrows arched. "I came in to buy some new rope, Miss Hathoway." He was irritated at having told a blatant lie.

"Oh." She stared at it. "Can you spin a loop and jump through it?"

He glared at her. "This," he said, hefting it irritably, "is nylon rope. It isn't worth a damn until you tie it between the back bumper of a truck and a fence-post and stretch it."

"You're kidding," she said.

"I am not." He moved closer, looking down at her. She was at least average height, but he still had to look down. She seemed very fragile somehow. Perhaps her life-style made her brittle.

He searched her soft eyes. "Did you drive in?" he asked so that she wouldn't know he'd followed her to town.

"Yes. With Winnie," she said. "She's trying on her wedding gown."

His thick eyebrow jerked. "The wedding will be Pryor's social event of the season," he said with faint sarcasm. He dragged a cigarette from his pocket and bent his dark head to light it. The thought of the wedding stung him. Dwight was a Nelson, truly his father's son. Dwight had inherited the lion's share of the business, even though Gene couldn't complain about his own inheritance. It was just that he'd been

the eldest son all his life. He'd belonged. Now he
didn't. Dwight and Winnie's wedding was a potent,
stinging reminder of that.

"It hurts you, doesn't it?"

The gentle question brought a silent gasp from his
lips. He stared down at her, caught completely off
guard by her unexpected remark. The compassion in
those eyes was like a body blow. She almost seemed
to glow with it. He couldn't have imagined anyone
looking at him like that a week ago, and he wasn't
sure he liked it even now.

"Haven't you got someplace to go, Miss Hathoway?" he asked irritably.

"I suppose that means you wish I did. Why are
you wearing bat-wing chaps in the northwest?" she
asked pleasantly. "And Mexican rowels?"

The cigarette poised halfway to his lips. "I used to
work down in Texas," he said hesitantly. "What do
you know about chaps?"

"Lots." She grinned. "I grew up reading Zane
Grey."

"No better teacher, except Louis L'Amour," he
murmured. His pale eyes slid down her body. She was
wearing jeans and a white knit shirt, short sleeved,
because it was June and warm.

"No hat," he observed, narrow-eyed. "You know
better, or you should, having lived in Arizona. June
is a hot month, even here."

She grimaced. "Yes, but I hate hats. It isn't usually
this warm, surely, this far north?"

Those hazel eyes were casting spells. He had to
drag his away. "We get hot summers. Winters are the

problem,'' he said, nodding toward the distant peaks, snow covered even in the summer. ''We get three and four feet of snow at a time. Trying to find calving cows in that can be a headache.''

''I expect so.'' Her eyes went to his thin mouth. ''But isn't summer a busier time?''

He looked down at her. ''Not as much so as April and September. That's when we round up cattle.''

''I guess that keeps you busy,'' she said softly.

''No more than anything else does,'' he said shortly. He had to get away from her. She disturbed him. ''I've got to go.''

''That's it, reject me,'' she said with a theatrical sigh, hiding her shyness in humor. ''Push me aside— I can take it.''

He smiled without meaning to. ''Can you?'' he murmured absently, lifting the cigarette to his lips.

''Probably not,'' she confessed dryly. She searched his eyes. ''Winnie warned me to stay away from you. She says you're a womanizer.''

He stared down at her. ''So? She's right,'' he said without pulling his punches. ''I've never made any secret of it.'' His eyes narrowed on her face. ''Did you expect a different answer?''

She shook her head. ''I'm glad I didn't get one. I don't mind the truth.''

''Neither do I, but we're pretty much in the minority. I find that most people prefer lies, however blatant.''

She felt momentarily guilty, because she was trying to behave like someone she wasn't. But she knew that her real self wasn't likely to appeal to him. She couldn't help herself.

Gene saw that expression come and go on her face and was puzzled by it. He glanced past her, watching Winnie in the doorway of a shop, talking to another woman.

"You'd better go," he said abruptly. "Your watchdog's about to spot you talking to me." He smiled with pure sarcasm. "She'll give you hell all day if she sees us together."

"Would you mind?" she asked.

He nodded. "For Dwight's sake, yes, I would. I don't want to alienate Winnie before the wedding." He laughed curtly. "Plenty of time for that afterward."

"You aren't half as bad as you pretend to be," she remarked.

He sobered instantly. "Don't you believe it, cupcake," he replied. "You'd better go."

"All right." She sighed, clutching the bag of thread against her breasts. "See you."

"Sure." He walked past her to his black Jeep and he didn't allow himself to look back. Pursuing her had been a big mistake. She was Winnie's best friend, and Winnie was obviously determined not to let her become one of his casual interludes. He had to keep his head. He had more than enough problems already, and alienating his future sister-in-law wasn't going to solve any of them. That being the case, it might be wise, he told himself sarcastically, if he stopped following her around!

Allison was calm by the time Winnie finally joined

her. "My dress is coming along beautifully," she said. "Did I see you talking to someone?"

"Just passing conversation. I got your mother's thread," Allison said, evading the curious question gracefully. By the time they got back to the car, Winnie had forgotten all about it.

But Allison couldn't forget about Gene. When she was invited, along with Winnie, to supper at the Nelson home two days later, it was almost as if Fate was working in her favor.

She wore a plain gray dress with a high neckline and straight skirt, gently gathered at the waist with a belt. It wasn't a sexy dress, but when she wore it, it became one. She did her hair in a neat French plait and put on makeup as Winnie had taught her. When she finished, she looked much less sophisticated than she had at the barbecue—a puzzling outcome.

"I don't look the way I did before," she told Winnie after they'd said good-night to Mrs. Manley and were on the way to the Nelsons'.

"You look great," Winnie corrected. "And tonight, will you please be yourself?"

"Why? Are you hoping that Gene Nelson might keep his distance if he sees what a frump I really am?" she murmured dryly.

"He seems to be doing that all by himself," Winnie reminded her. "I'm not trying to be difficult, honestly I'm not." She sighed worriedly. "I just don't want to see you hurt. Gene...isn't himself these days."

"What was he like before?" Allison asked softly.

Winnie laughed. "Full of fun. He always had his

eye on the ladies, but he was less blatant with it. Now, he's reckless and apparently without conscience when it comes to women. He doesn't really care whom he hurts.''

''I don't think he'd hurt me, though, Winnie,'' she said.

''Don't bet on it,'' the other woman replied. ''You put too much faith in people's better instincts. Some people don't have any.''

''I'll never believe that,'' Allison said firmly. ''Not after what I've seen. Beauty often hides in the most horrible places.''

Winnie's eyes were gentle as they glanced toward her friend. She didn't know what to say to Allison. Probably nothing would do much good. She'd just have to hope that Gene was out, or that, if he was home, he wasn't interested in Allison.

It was late afternoon, and still light. A gentle flutter of rain greeted them as they arrived in front of the Nelson house and darted up the steps to the front door.

''You're early,'' Marie stammered, flustered and wild-eyed when she opened the door for them. She swept back her blond hair. ''Oh, gosh, do either of you know anything about first aid? Dwight had to run to town for some wine, and Gene's ripped open his arm. I'm just hopeless…!''

''Where is he?'' Allison asked, her voice cool and professional-sounding. ''I know what to do.''

''Thank God!'' Marie motioned them along behind her, down the long hall toward the bedrooms.

''I think I'll wait in the living room, if you don't

mind.'' Winnie hesitated, grimacing. "I'm as hopeless as Marie is.''

"You won't be alone long," Marie promised her. "I can't stand the sight of blood, either! He's in there, Allison,'' she added, nodding toward an open bedroom door. "You can hear him from out in the hall.''

"I'll look after him," Allison assured her, leaving Marie to keep Winnie company while she ventured into the room.

Muttered curses were coming from the bathroom. Allison moved hesitantly past the antique furniture in the cream and brown confines of the room, certain that it was Gene's. The bed was king-size. There was a desk and chair in one corner and two chairs and a floor lamp in the other, beside a fireplace. The earth tones and Indian accent pieces suited what she knew of Gene Nelson.

But she didn't have time to study his taste in furnishings. She pushed open the bathroom door, which was already ajar, and walked in. The bathroom, like the bedroom, was done in beige and brown with a tile floor and a huge glass-fronted shower with gold fittings. There was a Jacuzzi, too. But it was the vanity sink that caught her eye. Gene was standing in front of it, in clothes similar to those he'd been wearing in town. His shirt was off and one brown, hair-roughened forearm was cut from elbow to wrist and dripping bright red blood into the marble sink.

"That needs stitching," she said.

He turned, his green eyes darker with pain, his lean face hard and without a smile. "What the hell do you want?'' he asked, irritated because he'd been thinking

of her when he'd gone too close to one of his few
horned cows and had his arm ripped for his pains.

"A Rolls and a house on the Riviera," she said.
She moved close, trying not to stare blatantly at the
broad, bronzed chest with its thick wedge of hair that
ran down his flat stomach and under the heavy brass
belt buckle that secured his jeans. He was beautifully
male, so striking that she had to drag her eyes away.

"You know what I mean," he returned shortly.

"Marie and your future sister-in-law are squea-
mish. I'm not. Let me see, please." She scanned the
things he'd dragged out of the medicine cabinet and
proceeded to gently bathe the long gash with soap and
water before she used a strong disinfectant and then
an antibiotic cream. "I guess you'll scream if I sug-
gest the local hospital emergency room?" she asked
as she worked.

He stared down at her bent dark head with mingled
emotions. He'd hoped to be gone before she and Winnie arrived, but he hadn't counted on letting his mind
wander and getting himself gored. "I've had worse
than this," he replied.

She looked up into his searching eyes, trying to
ignore the beat of her pulse and the difficulty she was
having with getting her breath. She was too involved
with hiding her own reactions to notice his racing
pulse and quick breathing. "At least it's stopped
bleeding. I don't suppose you have any butterfly bandages?"

"What?" he murmured, lost in her eyes.

"B...butterfly bandages," she stammered. She

dragged her eyes down to his forearm. "Never mind. I'll make do with these."

Her hands felt cool on his hot skin. He watched her work, marveling at the ease and confidence with which she put the dressing in place.

"You've done this before, haven't you?" he asked.

"Oh, yes," she said, smiling reminiscently. "Many times. I'm used to patching up people." She didn't add anything to that. It was too soon to talk about her past yet.

"You're good at it. That feels better."

"How did it happen?"

He chuckled softly. "I zigged when I should have zagged, cupcake. Now that you've gotten that one under control, care to have a go at this one?"

She put the last piece of adhesive in place and lifted her eyes. "Which one?" she asked.

He pointed to a smaller gash on his chest that was still bleeding.

"I guess your shirt was a total loss," she murmured dryly, trying to stop the trembling of her hands as she began to bathe the scratch. His chest was warm under her fingers, and she loved the feel of that thick hair as she worked through it to the cut. Her lips parted on quick, jerky breaths. He was hurt. She had to keep that in mind, and not let herself lose control like this.

"My shirt and the denim jacket I was wearing over it," he murmured. The feel of her hands on him was giving him problems. His body began to tense slowly as he watched her clean the cut. "If you try to put a bandage on that, I'm leaving,'' he added when she'd stopped the bleeding.

"I...I guess adhesive tape would hurt when it had to come out, with all that...hair,'' she faltered, her eyes helplessly tracing the muscular lines of his torso with involuntary delight.

The way she said it was faintly arousing. He ran a hand over the thick mass of it, nodding absently. "Just put some antiseptic on it, honey, and we'll let it go, okay?''

"Okay.'' *Honey.* No man had ever called her that in such a deep, sexy way, so that her toes curled inside her shoes. She took the antibiotic cream and put a little on her fingers. But when she began to rub it gently over the cut, he flinched and her fingers paused on his body.

"Did it hurt?'' she whispered, puzzled by the heavy beat of his heart under her hand and by the sudden fierce glitter of his eyes.

"Not the way you mean,'' he said curtly. He felt hot all over, and when she lifted her face, he could see the same awareness there. He couldn't let this happen, he told himself firmly. He had to stop it now.

But she smelled of flowers, and he loved the touch of those gentle hands on his bare skin. Involuntarily he traced her long, elegant fingers, simultaneously pressing them deeper into the hair on his chest so that they caressed the hard muscle. His eyes lifted to hers, holding them in a silence that was suddenly tense and hot with promise.

She looked younger tonight, in that gray dress with her hair in a braid at her back. Despite the makeup she'd used, she looked country fresh. He liked her better this way than in that sexy dress she'd worn at the barbecue. He almost said so, but he managed to bite back the comment in time.

"It's…stopped bleeding," she whispered. But she was looking into his eyes, not at the cut.

"So it has," he replied.

The hand that was caressing the back of hers moved her fingers slowly over a taut, flat male nipple, letting her feel the effect her touch was having on him. He pressed it close and hard, his whole hand covering hers as the silence continued.

She smelled leather and a faint breath of hay on him, pleasant scents that mingled with the after-shave he wore. Her heart was beating madly, and under her fingers she could feel the fierce pulsation of his own.

"Gene," she whispered unsteadily.

The sound of his name on her lips was his undoing. He couldn't help himself. He bent slowly, his eyes on her soft mouth, no other thought in his mind except possession.

His hands moved up to frame her face, warm and strong on her cheeks as he tilted her head to give him total access to her parted lips.

She didn't make even a pretense of resisting. Her hands rested lightly, with fascination, on the hard, warm contours of his chest, spearing into the thick mat of hair that covered it. She could taste his breath, smoky and warm, on her mouth, and she wanted him to kiss her with an almost feverish desperation. There had never been a man she'd felt this kind of attraction to. Just once she wanted to taste him. Just…once…

Her eyes closed. She stood on her tiptoes to coax his mouth the rest of the way while the world vanished around her. She heard the sharp intake of his breath and felt his hands contract and his mouth almost touched hers.

And just then a sharp, feminine voice broke into the tense silence with all the subtlety of an explosion.

Four

"Allison, is he all right?"

Winnie's voice hit Gene with the impact of a sledgehammer. He jerked back from Allison even as his hard mouth touched hers, his face going as rigid as the arousal he barely kept her from feeling.

He whirled away, grabbing his shirt and jacket. "Yes, he's all right," he called, irritated. He didn't know which bothered him the most—the interruption or his weakness.

"Oh. Sorry!" Winnie stammered.

There were fading footsteps. "My God, does she think I'm in any condition to ravish you?" he asked angrily, running a restless hand through his thick, straight hair.

Allison was still getting her breath back. She leaned against the vanity sink, her trembling hands behind her. "You don't understand," she said softly, wondering if she could find the right words to explain Winnie's protectiveness.

He turned, glancing at her irritably until his searching gaze fell to the taut nipples pressing against the soft fabric of her dress. His breath sighed out heavily. "Are you what you seem to be, Allison?" he asked unexpectedly, resignation in his tone. His eyes lifted back to capture hers. "Are you modern and sophisticated?"

"Why do you want to know?" she sidestepped the question.

His eyes narrowed and stabbed into hers. "Because there's no way on earth I'm getting involved with you if you aren't."

Her heart ran wild. "Do you want to get involved with me?" she asked huskily.

"My God, can't you tell?" he demanded. His chest rose and fell roughly. "I've barely touched you, and I'm on fire!"

That made two of them, but she didn't imagine he could tell how she felt. She wanted to get close to him. If she told him the truth, he wouldn't come near her. If she kept her secret, there was a slight chance that he might drop his guard, that she might get to see the real man, the hurting one. As for anything more, perhaps they could agree to some ground rules that would protect her until she could tell him the truth.

"I'm not modern enough to jump into bed with any man who asks," she said simply, and met his eyes bravely. "I like to know what I'm getting into first."

His chin lifted with faint arrogance. "You're cautious, then. So am I. I won't rush you. But I don't want a platonic relationship."

"Neither do I," she said, but with her eyes averted.

He hesitated. Something didn't ring true about what she was saying, but he couldn't quite put his finger on it. He wondered if this wasn't lunacy. A woman was the last complication he needed right now, and he hadn't forgotten that her best friend was marrying his brother. There were at least ten good reasons for keeping his distance, but none of them mattered when he was around Allison. He seemed to have been alone for a very long time. When he was with her, the aching loneliness vanished.

"Suppose we go to a movie tomorrow night?" he asked.

"Winnie won't like it."

"I'm not asking Winnie," he replied easily. "Or anyone else. Just you and me."

"Could we go to Cody? Isn't there a rodeo there every night?"

He smiled slowly. "Every night during the summer," he corrected. "We'll save that for another time. But we can detour through Cody, if you like. The nearest movie house is in Billings."

"Montana?" she exclaimed. "But that's over a hundred miles away!"

"No distance at all out here, cupcake."

"I suppose not. It's like that in Arizona, too, but I'd forgotten." She stared at him quietly, her heart still beating wildly. "I guess you supply animals to the rodeo in Cody, too?"

He nodded. "That one and any number of others."
He studied her for a long moment. "You'd better get
out of here. I need a shower before we eat."

"All right."

"Unless you'd like to stay and scrub my back?"
he mused, a wicked gleam in his eyes.

"It's much too early for that sort of thing," she
told him and left with a demure glance from under
her lashes.

He was smiling when she left the room, but she
wasn't. She wondered what she was letting herself in
for, and how she thought she was going to keep a
man like that at bay. If he really was the womanizer
everyone said he was, she'd be in over her head in
no time.

"He's as good as new," Allison assured the two
women when she joined them in the living room.
"Almost, anyway. The cut on his arm really needed
stitching, but he won't go to a doctor."

"That's Gene," Marie said wearily. "It's been so
hard for him. I wish Dad had never left that letter. It
would have been so much kinder not to have told him
after such a long time. Let's go on into the dining
room. Gene won't be long, I'm sure, and we can drink
coffee while we talk."

She led them into the dining room, where a cherry
table was set under an elegant crystal chandelier. The
floor was oak, highly polished, and the walls were
wood paneled. It was the most elegant room Allison
had seen in years. They sat down and busied themselves with coffee for several minutes before Allison
finally voiced the question that had been nagging her.

"Why did your father leave a note for Gene?" she asked curiously.

Marie shook her head. "Nobody knows. Dad was honest to a fault, and he was a deep thinker. Maybe he thought Gene had the right to know. His real father is still alive, even if Gene would rather die than go to see him. Heritage, health, so many things depend on knowing who your real parents are. I think that he planned to tell Gene before he died. That would have been Dad's way. He certainly wouldn't have wanted him to find out the way he did. It's hurt Gene so badly."

"I suppose it's been difficult for you and Dwight, too," Allison said gently.

"You can't imagine. We don't care who Gene's real dad is. Gene is our brother and we love him. But he can't accept that," Marie said. "He's still trying to come to grips with it. I wonder sometimes if he ever will. Meanwhile, he's just hell to live with."

"Is he staying for supper?" Winnie asked with a worried glance at Allison.

"Yes," Allison said. "At least he said he was."

"Don't look so worried," Marie told Winnie, grinning at her expression. "He'll be nice because Allison's here. I think he likes her."

"God forbid!" Winnie said. "You know how he is with women!"

"He won't hurt Allison," Marie said. "Don't be such a worrywart."

"I hope you're right. Anyway," Winnie sighed, "he's involved with Dale, isn't he?"

"No, he isn't," Gene said from the doorway. He

lifted an eyebrow at Winnie's shocked face as he joined them, freshly showered and shaved, dressed in a knit shirt and dark slacks. He looked wickedly handsome, and Allison's heart raced at the sight of him.

"Sorry," Winnie began.

Gene lifted a careless hand, stopping her before she got started. "I'm not going to gobble up your houseguest," he said quietly. "But she'll be safer with me than some of the other yahoos around here, especially at night," he added with a meaningful stare. "I'll take care of her."

"Okay. I suppose you're right." Winnie sighed softly. "It's just that..." She glanced toward Allison, grimacing. "Well..."

"She's your best friend," Gene finished for her with a faint smile. "No problem. I won't hurt her, Winnie."

"Will you stop?" Allison asked Winnie on an exasperated laugh. "I'm twenty-five."

"Yes, but..."

"What are we having for dinner?" Allison interrupted, arching her eyebrows at an amused Marie.

"Duck," Marie returned. "And if I don't take the orange sauce out of the microwave, we'll be having it without sauce! Excuse me."

Before Winnie could say anything else to Gene and Allison, Dwight was back with the wine. But all through dinner, Gene's eyes kept darting to Allison's, as hers did to him. Whatever there was between them, it was explosive and mutual. She hoped she wouldn't have cause to regret giving it a chance.

Over dinner, she learned that Gene was a wizard

with figures and that his taste in books ran to mysteries and biographies, while he took a conservative stand on politics and a radical one on ecology. She discovered that he enjoyed a lot of the same things she did, like winter sports and the Winter Olympics, not to mention science fiction movies. He was droll and faintly sarcastic, but underneath there had to be a sensitive caring man. Allison wanted to flush him out.

He pulled her aside while Winnie was saying goodnight to Dwight and Marie.

"I'll pick you up at five tomorrow afternoon," he said. "We'll need to get an early start. It's a long drive."

"You're sure you want to?"

"No," he said curtly, and meant it. He'd never wanted involvement with her, but things seemed to be out of his hands for once. Out of control, like his life. He shifted his stance, putting the past away from him. "We'll have dinner in Billings," he continued, searching her eyes slowly, "before the movie starts. There's a nice restaurant in the Sheraton."

"Okay." She smiled shyly. "I'll look forward to it."

He only nodded. He didn't want to admit how easily he could echo that sentiment. In the past, being a loner had had distinct advantages. He didn't want to have to account for his time or have restraints put on his freedom. Dale had tried that tack, and Jessie, God bless her, was as thick as a plank. One smile and Jessie was hearing wedding bells.

Allison's soft voice caught his attention again and

he glanced to where she and Winnie were laughing with Marie over some television program they'd apparently all seen as they said good-night at the front door.

He waved in their general direction and went up to his room. He wondered if Winnie was going to talk Allison out of tomorrow's date. If she did, it might be the best thing for both of them, he decided.

But Winnie didn't manage that, despite the fact that she coaxed and pleaded all the way home that night.

"Your reputation...!" she concluded finally, using one last desperate argument.

"It will survive one or two dates," Allison said firmly. "Oh, Winnie, he's so alone! Can't you see it? Can't you see the pain in his eyes, the emptiness?"

Winnie pulled up in front of her house, turned off the engine and the lights with a long sigh. "No. I don't suppose I'm blessed with your particular kind of empathy. But you don't know what it's like with an experienced man. You've hardly even dated, and Gene has been around. If you drop your guard for a minute, he'll seduce you, you crazy little trusting idiot!"

"It takes two," Allison reminded her.

"Yes, and I can see sparks flying between the two of you the minute you're together! Allie, it's an explosive chemistry and you don't have the faintest idea how helpless you'd be if he turned up the heat!"

"Aren't you forgetting how my parents brought me up?" Allison asked gently.

"No, I'm not," Winnie replied tersely. "But I'm telling you that ideals and principles have a breaking point. Sexual attraction is physical, and the mind doesn't have a lot of control over it.''

"I can say no," Allison replied. "Now let's go and watch some television. Okay?"

Winnie started to speak, but she realized it was going to be futile. It was like trying to explain surfing to an Eskimo. She could only hope that Allie's resolve was equal to Gene Nelson's ardor when it was put to the test.

Gene pulled up in the yard at exactly five o'clock the next afternoon. He was wearing gray slacks with a gray patterned Western shirt and a bola tie, a matching gray Stetson atop his head and hand-tooled gray boots on his feet. He looked elegant, and Allison's heart skipped when he came in the front door behind Winnie.

She looked good, he mused. She had on a pretty lilac shirtwaist dress with a flowery scarf, and her hair was loose, hanging down her back like a wavy dark curtain almost to her waist. The dress clung gently to her slender body in just the right places, enhancing her firm, high breasts and narrow waist. She had it buttoned up right to her throat, but it only made the fit more sexy to Gene, who assumed that the prim fashion statement was a calculated one. He smiled gently, liking her subtle gesture.

Allison, unaware of his thoughts, smiled back. "Is this dressy enough, or should I wear something else?" she asked. "I'm not used to fancy restaurants."

"You look fine," Gene assured her.

"Indeed you do. Have fun," Winnie said gently.

She glanced at Gene. "Take care of her," she said worriedly.

"No sweat." He linked Allison's soft hand in his and led her out the door, leaving an unconvinced Winnie behind.

"Why is she so protective of you?" Gene asked when they were out on the main highway in his sleek black Jeep.

Allison studied him from the comparative safety of her deep bucket seat. "She thinks you're too experienced for me."

He raised an eloquent eyebrow. "Am I, cupcake?" he asked with cynical mockery.

She laughed softly. "Probably. But you don't scare me."

"Give me time." He lifted the cigarette he'd lit to his mouth and inhaled. "You haven't asked which movie I'm taking you to."

"No, I haven't. Is it a good one?"

He cracked a window to let the smoke out of the cab. "I don't know. I don't see movies too much these days. This one is supposed to be about the cattle business. But if it follows the trend, it'll be about people taking their clothes off to discuss gene splicing and cloning of pedigree cattle."

She laughed involuntarily at the disgust in his voice. "You don't think much of modern films, I gather?"

"I loved the Indiana Jones trilogy," he replied. "I've seen all the series science-fiction movies, and I thought *Gandhi* and *Born on the Fourth of July* and *The Color Purple* were the best of the best. Sex," he added with a glance in her direction, "should not be a spectator sport."

"No," she agreed, averting her eyes to the darkening skyline. She was glad of the dimly lit interior of the Jeep, so that he couldn't see the slight embarrassment the remark caused her.

They drove in silence for a few minutes. He took a detour to let her see a bit more of Wyoming, going north and west several miles out of the way so that she could see one of the area's most fascinating sights.

When he mentioned that they were traveling through Shoshone Canyon, Allison didn't need to be told that, because the eerie sound of the wind and the gnarled outcroppings of rock in their desert colors gave her cold chills. She remembered what Winnie had said about the area, and she almost asked Gene about it, but the tunnel through the mountain came into view ahead and her curiosity vanished in sheer fascination at the engineering job it must have been to put that long tunnel through solid rock.

Once they were through the tunnel, it was just a little way into Cody. Gene pointed out the famous Buffalo Bill Cody museum and the rodeo grounds on the way through the small city, adding that one of the first water systems in the West had been funded by Bill Cody with labour provided by the Mormons.

"Why, this looks like southern Arizona!" Allison exclaimed as she looked out the window when they were driving north out of Cody.

"Yes, it does," he said. "But when we go through the Pryor Mountains and head into Montana you'll see the difference in the terrain. Wyoming is mostly jagged mountains, and southern Montana is mostly buttes and rolling grassland.'' He smiled at her. "I love both. I could happily spend the rest of my life in Billings, but I suppose I've gotten too used to Wyoming."

"Where were you born?" she asked.

His face hardened and his lean hands gripped the wheel convulsively. "My birth certificate says Billings, Montana," he replied tersely. "I suppose that's where my mother and her...husband lived at the time." He didn't add that he'd never had occasion to look at his birth certificate in all those years—even when he'd joined the service, his mother had provided records to the authorities. Why hadn't he ever questioned it? It wasn't until after Hank Nelson died that he'd seen all the paperwork—the birth certificate with the name he was born under and the adoption papers. God, it hurt to realize how easily he'd accepted the lies....

Allison hesitated. She could tell that it was like putting a knife into him to answer the question. But his own avoidance of the subject had surely added to his discomfort.

"You don't like to talk about it, do you?" she asked quietly.

"No," he said honestly.

"When a splinter gets under the skin," she began carefully, "pulling it out at once prevents it from doing too much damage. But when it's left inside, it festers and causes infection."

His eyes sliced through her. "And that's what my past is, do you think? A splinter that's embedded?"

"In a manner of speaking," she replied. Her eyes fell to the firm set of his lips. "I imagine it was the shock of your life to find out who your father was in such a way. But I agree with Marie. I think your stepfather meant to tell you and kept putting it off until it was too late."

His pale green eyes flashed. He didn't like being reminded of it, but what she said made sense. It was just the newness of discussing it, he supposed. He wouldn't let Marie or Dwight talk about it around him. He couldn't really understand why he hadn't already cut Allison dead. He knew instinctively that she was sensitive enough that one hard word would stop her. He just couldn't seem to speak that one hard word. The idea of hurting her didn't appeal to him at all.

They drove into Billings, along the wide, uncrowded streets, and Gene pointed out the Sheraton—easy to find from any direction, he added, because it was the tallest building in town.

"The airport sits on the Rimrocks," he added, nodding toward his left as they turned toward the Sheraton. "Yellowstone Kelly's buried up there, and the old graveyard is down the hill from the grave."

"I'll bet you could spend a whole day just looking around Billings," she remarked as she noted the spacious outlay of the city. Far in the distance was what looked like an oil refinery, and there were railroad tracks right through the city.

"Billings is big, all right," he agreed, his eyes on

a traffic light up ahead. "And the surrounding area is full of history."

"Yes, I know," she said excitedly. "The Custer Battlefield is somewhere nearby, isn't it?"

"Over near Hardin," he said. "I'll take you there one day if you like."

Her heart jumped. He made it sound as if they were headed for a real relationship, not just a quick flirtation. She stared at his profile with a feeling of slow warmth building inside her.

"I'd like that very much, Gene," she said softly.

He was grateful that the traffic light changed in time to distract him, because the expression on her face could have hypnotized him. He'd never seen such warmth in a woman's eyes. It drew him like a blazing fire on a snowy night.

"You shouldn't look at me that way when I'm trying to drive," he said curtly.

"I beg your pardon?"

He glanced at her as he pulled into the Sheraton's parking lot, mentally praying for an empty spot. She looked blank, as if the remark didn't register.

"Never mind," he murmured, his keen eyes on the last space, where a car was backing out. "The answer to a prayer," he chuckled.

"The parking spot?"

"You bet," he agreed. "The food here is something special, as you'll see, so it's usually crowded on weekends."

He pulled into the vacated parking spot and parked. The night air was warm and the city smelled of anything but exhaust fumes. Perhaps it was its very spaciousness.

"This doesn't look like Arizona, but it's just as spread out," she remarked, staring around her with interest.

"Most Western cities are," he said. He escorted her into the lobby and then into the elevator. They rode up to the restaurant near the top of the building and were seated by a window overlooking the Yellowstone River and the railroad tracks. A freight train was barreling through the darkness and Allison's eyes followed it wistfully.

"Do you like trains?" he asked, glancing down at the passing train.

"Oh, yes," she said with a sigh. "I used to dream about having an electric train set of my very own, when I was little. But I was taught that there were many things more important than toys."

He smiled gently. "Such as?"

She returned the smile. "A pair of shoes for a neighbor's little girl who didn't have any. Glasses for a seamstress who was the sole support of three children. Insulin for a diabetic who could barely afford to pay rent."

He had to search for words. He hadn't expected that reply. "Taught by whom? Your parents?"

She nodded. She looked down, toying with her utensils. "They were...very special people." She had to bite down hard to keep the tears back. Nightmare memories flashed through her mind.

Gene didn't miss the sudden look of panic on her face. His lean hand crossed the table and caught hers, enveloping it tightly. "You can tell me about it later," he said quietly.

His compassion startled her. Her lips parted as she met his pale green eyes and searched them, while her fingers curled trustingly into his. "It's still fresh, you see," she whispered huskily.

"You lost them recently?"

She nodded. Words couldn't get past the lump in her throat.

"So that's why you're here," he said, thinking aloud. "And why Winnie's so protective of you."

She didn't disagree. There was so much more to it than that, but she couldn't talk about it just yet. Instead her fingers curled against the firm, comforting strength of his.

"If it helps, I know what you're going through," he said. His voice was as comforting as his clasp. "You'll get past it. Take it one day at a time and give yourself room to grieve. Don't shut it inside."

She took a steadying breath and forced a smile. "Look who's telling whom not to shut it inside," she said, meeting his gaze.

He laughed softly. "Okay. Point taken." The smile faded and he frowned with real concern as he studied her wan face. "Want to give this a miss and go back to Winnie's?"

Her lips parted. "Oh, no, please," she faltered. "I'm okay. It was just…sometimes I think about them and it hurts. I'm sorry. I didn't mean to spoil your evening."

"What makes you think you have?" he asked quietly. "I know how it feels to hurt inside. You don't have to hide it from me."

She took a steadying breath and smiled. "Thank you."

He shrugged. "No sweat. Are you hungry?"

She laughed. "Yes."

"Good. So am I."

Their waitress made an appearance, almost running to keep up with the demands on her, apologetic as she deposited a menu and then took their order. Gene found that Allison shared his taste in food, because she ordered a steak and salad and coffee, just as he had. He grinned.

"Coffee will poison you," he reminded her after the waitress had left it and gone off to the kitchen.

She put cream and sugar into hers. "As long as it doesn't cripple me, I'll be okay," she said. "You're drinking it, too," she pointed out.

"Of course. I didn't say it would poison *me*."

Her face beamed as she studied him. "I noticed."

He grinned at her. "I hope you also noticed that I'm not smoking."

"It's hard to miss," she confided. "You're turning purple."

"I'll survive until we get outside again," he replied. "Besides, here comes our food."

Sure enough, the waitress brought their orders and then they were too busy eating to talk. Allison hadn't realized how hungry she was. She ate, but, with every bite, her eyes were helplessly on Gene Nelson's dark face.

Five

The theater wasn't crowded, so Gene and Allison had a whole row to themselves, away from the few other people in the audience. Gene put his Stetson atop one folded seat and stretched his long legs, crossing one over the other while the previews ran. Allison munched the popcorn he'd bought her and tried to pay attention to the screen.

It had been a long time since she'd seen a movie, because there hadn't even been a television set where she and her parents had spent the past few years. She was behind the times in a lot of ways, and the fact was really brought home to her as the story unfolded. As Gene had predicted, despite the fact that the story was supposed to deal with cattle ranching, most of it seemed to take place in bedrooms. She watched, red-faced, during one particular scene replete with heavy breathing and explicit material.

Gene glanced at her expression with faint curiosity. That wide-eyed gape couldn't be for real. Nobody who had a television set could be shocked these days. Of course, it could be seeing a scene like this with him, a comparative stranger, that made her nervous. She might not be all that experienced, even if she'd been with one or two men. Funny how it disturbed him to think of her being with any man at all except himself.

He reached for her hand and drew it gently into his, resting it on his muscular thigh. She resisted for a few seconds, until the contact began to weaken her and she gave in.

His long fingers played with hers, teasing between them while things heated up on the screen. He lifted them to his lips and began to nibble at her fingertips with slow, sensual intent.

Allison had never been exposed to this kind of thing. She felt his lips against her fingers and almost gasped at the sensations she felt when he nibbled them.

She tried to draw back her hand, but he held it in a firm, gentle grasp. What was happening now on the screen had her rigid with disbelief.

Gene glanced down at Allison, watching her reaction to the screen. Her expression was one of astonished awe, and something scratched at the back of his mind, only to be gone before he could let it in. Her fingers clenched around his unconsciously and he returned the pressure.

"Amazing what they can get away with, isn't it?" he murmured deeply, keeping his voice low. The nearest people were three rows away, so there was little danger of being overheard. His thumb rubbed slowly across her damp palm, pressing the back of her hand into the powerful muscle of his thigh. The sensation rocked him, because it was such an innocent contact. He looked back at the screen, all too aware of her warm touch. His chest rose and fell heavily as he watched the couple on the screen. "Does it embarrass you?" he asked quietly.

"Yes," she moaned, giving in to honesty.

"I thought you said you were a modern girl," he murmured, and he smiled, but it was a kind smile.

"I thought you said sex shouldn't be a spectator sport," she returned.

He chuckled at the riposte. "Touché." The screen suddenly drew their attention as the sounds grew louder and more frantic and finally ended in breathless cries of simulated ecstasy.

Allison was almost trembling by now. Gene felt stirred himself. It had been a while between women. He looked down at Allison with fascination as he felt the shiver go through her. She had to be very sensitive to react so fiercely to a love scene.

His hand absently moved hers up his thigh, until he realized what he was doing and felt the almost frantic restraint of her hand.

"Sorry," he murmured dryly as he released her fingers and watched them retreat to her lap. "I guess it got to me more than I realized."

"They shouldn't show things like that," she faltered, still red-faced and unsteady.

"I couldn't agree more. I didn't realize it would be this explicit." He stood and tugged her along with him, ignoring the curious glances of much younger couples.

"They think we're crazy to leave, don't they?" she asked as they walked through the lobby to gain the street.

"No doubt. But they're a different generation. Come to think of it," he added as they reached the dark sidewalk, "so are you."

"I'm only nine years younger than you are," she protested.

He smiled down at her, the coolness of the night air calming his heated blood. "Almost a generation, these days," he observed. He slid his hand into hers and clasped it gently, his head lifting as he heard the first strains of Mozart in the distance. "If you don't care for explicit sex, how about soft music and ice cream?"

"Soft music?"

"There's an ice-cream social, complete with orchestra concert, in the park on summer nights," he explained. "Come on. I'll show you."

He helped her into the car and drove down to the enormous city park she'd seen earlier, with its ancient towering cottonwood trees and lush grass. Tables and chairs were set up for visitors, although plenty of the guests were sprawled on blankets or quilts on the dry grass. It was like something out of a fantasy, and Allison was enchanted.

"How delightful!" she exclaimed.

Gene lifted an eyebrow and smiled as he led her from the car into the throng, past where the symphony orchestra played magnificently. This was very much his kind of affair, and it touched him that Allison should find it so enjoyable, which she very obviously did.

"I have to admit that this is much more my scene than risqué movies," he mused. "Doing it is one thing, but watching other people do it—or pretend to—doesn't really appeal to me."

She averted her eyes, clinging to his strong lean hand as he led her to one of the tables where home-made ice cream was being dished up.

"I guess you know enough about it already, if what people say about your reputation is true," she said quietly when they were standing in line.

He turned to look down at her, worldly knowledge in his pale eyes. "Are you fishing for a denial?" he asked in a voice that sent goose bumps down her spine. "What they say about me is true. I've never made any secret of it. I've just been a little less discreet in the past few months."

She felt nervous. He'd never looked more like a predator, and she was feeling more threatened by the minute.

He moved closer to her as the line caught up and surged forward. His reputation had never bothered him before. It bothered him when Allison looked at him in that threatened way. "What about you?" he asked just above her ear. "You don't talk about your private life very much."

"There's not a lot to tell," she confessed.

His lean hand traced her shoulder lazily, an action calculated to disturb her. It didn't fail. Her breath caught audibly, and he felt a surge of desire for her that made his knees go weak.

"I don't believe that." He caught her waist with both hands and held her lightly in front of him while the queue moved ever closer to the ice cream. "What flavor do you like?"

"Vanilla," she said at once, because whenever that rare treat had been available, vanilla was invariably all that was offered.

"I like chocolate myself."

"Most men do, I think," she recalled with a smile, remembering how her charges, even the oldest of them, grumbled about the lack of that flavor.

His fingers tightened. "Something you know from experience?"

She put her hands over his to support them. "I suppose, in a way," she agreed.

"How experienced are you?" he asked.

"That's a question a gentleman doesn't ask," she chided, trying to make a joke out of it. And fortunately, before he could pursue the matter, they reached the ice cream.

The orchestra played many familiar pieces, and Allison found herself sitting beside Gene on the grass on a quilt they'd borrowed from a younger couple nearby.

Gene had mentioned that they'd come up from Wyoming, and the young man—much thinner and fairer than Gene—had grinned and asked, "Came up especially for the music, did you?"

"To tell you the truth, we came up for a movie," Gene replied ruefully. "But we left."

The young woman, a vivid redhead, put her hands over her mouth and giggled with a shy glance at her companion. "The one that's playing tonight?" she asked.

"That's right," Gene agreed.

"We left, too," she said in a very country-sounding drawl. "My daddy would skin me alive if he knew I'd been to such a film, so I made Johnny leave. He liked it," she added with another meaningful look.

"It's life," the boy replied. "We're getting married in two months, after all, Gertie."

"Johnny!" She went scarlet and jumped up. "I'll get us some more ice cream!"

"Virgins," Johnny sighed and then smiled with pure joy.

That smile bothered Gene. He'd never known a virgin, not in all his life. He'd certainly never dated one. But part of him envied that young boy, to be going into a marriage with a woman who'd saved such a precious part of her life for him. He'd never have to wonder about his wife's ex-lovers or how he compared, because there hadn't been any. He'd be the only one, at first anyway, and all her first times would be with him.

He looked down at Allison with speculation. How would it be, he wondered, if she were that fresh and untouched? His eyes ran slowly down her body and he tried to picture himself with her in bed, slowly teaching her things he'd learned. Would she be shocked? Or would it all be old hat to her? He'd found that experienced women tended to be inventive in bed, and uninhibited. That was a definite plus. But it must have been special, too, to be able to teach those responses to a woman, to touch her and hear her cry out with pleasure and know that no other man had ever seen or heard her in ecstasy.

The thoughts bothered him. Surely Allison was experienced, at her age, and she could certainly flirt with the best of them. He sighed. Anyway, what could he expect from a casual interlude like she was going to be? It was just going to be sex, nothing more, and daydreams had no part in this.

As the music built and the last of the ice cream began to disappear, Gene suddenly became aware of time. It was almost a three-hour drive back to Pryor at night, and they were going to be later than he'd expected.

"I hate this, but we have to go," he told Allison after checking his watch. "We've got a long drive back."

"We saw your Jeep," Johnny remarked. He smiled. "Nice wheels. We're starting out in a '56 pickup. But it's tough," he added, "and that's what you need on a ranch."

"Tell me about it." Gene grinned. "We've got a '55 Ford pickup that I still use to haul calves. Nothing wrong with a classic vehicle."

Johnny beamed. "You bet!"

Gene shrugged. "Starting out is fun. Everybody does it."

"You two married?" Gertie asked.

"No chance," Gene chuckled. "She'd run a mile if I asked her."

"Too bad. You look good together." Gertie leaned against Johnny with love beaming out of her face as she looked up at him.

"So do you two," Allison said gently. "God bless."

"You, too."

"Thanks for the loan of the quilt," Gene added, neatly folding it before handing it back. He didn't want to think about how he and Allison looked together, and marriage was the last thing on his mind. He was glad Allison hadn't made an issue of his reply to Johnny's question. She seemed almost relieved that he'd made a joke of it. Maybe she was marriage-shy, too. That would make things easier.

"Our pleasure. Drive carefully."

Gene nodded. He took Allison's hand and walked her back to the Jeep.

"That was fun," she said. "Thank you."

He looked down at her. "We'll do it again sometime," he said noncommittally.

He opened the passenger door for her, but as she moved into the space he'd made, he turned unexpectedly so that his body was touching hers, one hand holding the door, the other on the cab, so that she was trapped.

"I like the dress," he said. "Lilac suits you."

"Thank you," she replied. His proximity was

working on her like a drug. She felt her breath catch as she drank in the clean, cologne-scented warmth of his tall, fit body close to hers.

He bent one leg, so that his knee brushed past her thigh to rest against the seat. The contact brought him even closer, his body shielding her from onlookers in the park.

His breath was warm as his head bent, his glittery eyes meeting hers in the light from the park. "I'll be too busy for a few days, but on the weekend we could go sightseeing up around the Custer Battlefield. And next Tuesday night, we'll go up to Cody for the rodeo if you like."

"Yes," she said without hesitation. She searched his lean, dark face with pure pleasure. "I'd like that very much." Allison was surprised at the effect he had on her. He wasn't even touching her and her body was tingling.

He smiled, because he could read her expression very well indeed. He bent a little closer, so that she could feel his breath on her mouth. She could almost taste him.

"So would I, cupcake," he said softly. He let his eyes drop deliberately to her mouth and stared at it until he heard her breath catch and saw her lips part in helpless response. He leaned just a little closer. "We'd better go," he whispered, letting his breath brush her mouth. It was exciting to tease her; she responded to it so deliciously. She made him feel like the first man who'd done this with her, and his ego soared.

Just as she was beginning to tremble with anticipation, he drew back slowly, still smiling, and gently handed her into the cab. As he went around to the driver's side, his eyes gleamed with unholy delight. He knew she was his anytime he wanted her. The one advantage of experience was that it could recognize capitulation. He was going to stay away from her for a few days and build the tension between them before he made another move. Calculation, surely, but it would be for her benefit, too. Their first time would be explosive.

He got in and started the Jeep. "It'll warm up in a minute," he said, watching her wrap her arms around her breasts.

She smiled thankfully, trying to hide her nervousness. "I didn't think it would get chilly at night."

"Now you know."

"I sure do!" she agreed with a laugh, and shivered until the heater began to blow warm air.

She leaned her head back against the seat and Gene turned on a country-and-western radio station. The drive back to Pryor was very pleasant, despite the fact that they talked very little. She felt safe with him. Comfortable and safe, even through the excitement he generated in her. She wondered if earlier he'd wanted to kiss her and had drawn back because of the crowd. Or was he playing with her? She didn't know. She sighed silently, wishing she had just a little more experience of men to draw on.

They pulled up at the Manley house. It was dark, except for the porch light, and when Allison glanced at the Jeep's clock, she was amazed to find it was three o'clock in the morning.

"I told you we'd be late getting home," Gene mused, watching her catch her breath as she looked toward the dash. "At least they don't seem to be worried about you," he added, nodding toward the darkened windows.

"Don't you believe it," she replied with a gentle smile. "The lights may be off, but I'll bet Winnie isn't asleep. She's like a mother hen sometimes."

He turned in his seat and unfastened her seat belt and then his, leaning back as one dark hand went out to tease the hair at her throat lazily. "Do you need one?" he laughed softly.

She felt her body tingle. All evening it had been a war of nerves with him, from the way he'd played with her hand in the theater to the way he'd looked at her in the park and that almost-kiss as he'd helped her into the Jeep to come home. Now she was at fever pitch, and she wanted his mouth more than she'd ever imagined she could want anything.

"No, I...don't think so," she said unsteadily. Her eyes fell to his mouth hungrily.

He saw that rapt stare and his heart jumped. She was easy to read for a sophisticated woman. Perhaps it was the first time she'd reacted so strongly to a prospective lover, and that made him proud. It was one thing to turn a virgin's head, but quite another to make an experienced woman nervous and unsure of herself.

His fingers moved to her cheek and traced it lightly and then settled at her jaw while his thumb dragged across her soft mouth in a savagely arousing motion.

She actually gasped, her eyes widening as they met his in the dim light from the dash.

"You don't wear much makeup, do you?" he asked deeply. The feel of her mouth was exciting to him. His thumb rubbed more insistently at her lips, parting them against the pearly white of her teeth. "I'm glad. I don't like layers of lipstick on a woman's mouth when I kiss it."

She felt hot all over. Winnie had warned her about Gene Nelson's expertise and she hadn't understood. Now, suddenly, she began to. She wanted to pull his fingers away from her mouth, she wanted to pull them closer, she wanted to run!

He saw and felt that reaction, registering it with a little curiosity and a lot of pride. He smiled softly as he caught a handful of her long hair with his other hand and pulled her face under his with easy mastery.

"Bite me," he breathed as his mouth dragged against hers in brief, arousing kisses. She tasted mint and coffee and ice cream and pure man as he played on her attraction to him in the smouldering silence that followed. She couldn't breathe properly. Her fingers bit into his broad shoulders, feeling the steely tautness of the warm muscle as his teeth nibbled at her lower lip.

He lifted his head a fraction and looked into her dazed hazel eyes, his own pale green ones bright with arousal. "Bite me," he repeated gruffly, his fingers contracting in her hair to force her face back up to his. "I like it rough," he breathed into her open mouth. "Don't you?"

She didn't know how she liked it or what he expected of her. She could barely think at all and the words didn't really register. She moved closer, not needing the impetus of his strong hand in her hair to force the movement. She felt him stiffen a little as she slid her arms around his neck with a helpless moan and pushed her mouth hard against his.

The kiss was sweet and heady. His lips parted hungrily and he pressed her head back into his shoulder with the sheer force of his ardor. He made a sound deep in his throat. The taste of her was making him drunk. He couldn't remember the last time he'd felt like this in a woman's arms. Her soft, eager response tested his control to the limits. For an experienced woman, she was purely lacking in seductive skills, unless this rapt submission to his mouth was some kind of feminine tactic.

At any rate, he was too involved to care. He shifted her, bringing her across his hard thighs to lie in his arms while his mouth began to invade hers.

She struggled faintly and he drew away, his breath shuddering out against her moist, swollen lips.

"What is it?" he asked, his voice almost betraying him with its deep, drowsy huskiness.

She swallowed, trembling at the feel of his hard thighs under her. Something had happened to him while they were kissing, something masculine that was totally out of her experience, and she was shy and a little frightened.

When she tried to shift away, he understood, but he only smiled mockingly. "Is this a problem?" he murmured, one steely hand pressing at the base of her spine to hold her against his raging arousal.

She gasped and stiffened in his arms.

"Too much too soon, Allison?" he murmured, his pale green eyes narrowing as they met hers. "At any rate, I can't help it."

"Please," she said, flustered, and tried again to move away. He held her, firmly but gently. She knew she probably sounded like an outraged virgin—but that was what she was.

"You're twenty-five," he said solemnly. "Too old for little-girl games." His hand contracted again, deliberately, and he watched her face flush, her eyes widen. Odd, that reaction, because it actually seemed genuine. Not that it could be. He refused to believe that.

"Gene," she protested breathlessly, because incredibly the evidence of his need kindled something comparable in her. She'd never felt that knotting in her lower belly, the rush of warmth, the weak trembling that made her helpless.

He bent toward her, his lips poised just above hers, tempting them. He whispered something then, something so explicit and softly threatening that she actually gasped. When her lips parted, his moved sensuously between them, his tongue probing tenderly past her teeth as if to emphasize what he'd just said to her.

The combination of seductive whisper and equally seductive action tore a shocked moan from her throat. What he was doing to her mouth was...outrageous! Crude, and suggestive and...

She shivered. Her eyes opened to find him watching her while his tongue probed and withdrew in a soft, gentle, subtly arousing rhythm that she was utterly helpless to resist.

And while his tongue touched and tasted, one lean hand was riding up her rib cage to tease around a swollen breast. Even through three layers of fabric, the sensation was devastating. He held her gaze the whole while, intoxicated with the way she responded to it, with the look on her face, the shocked, almost terrified fascination in her misty, dilated eyes. When his thumb suddenly stroked her taut nipple she shuddered and moaned sharply.

He lifted his head, because he liked that. He wanted to see if he could make it happen again. And he did. Again and again, the sound of his fingers faintly abrasive against the fabric of her bodice unnaturally loud in the cab of the Jeep. His hand became more insistent on her soft body, openly caressing now as she gasped for breath and stiffened in his arms, lying helplessly against him and without resistance.

"Yes, it feels good, doesn't it?" he breathed, pride and faint arrogance in the way he was watching her. "You're very, very aroused, little Allison," he said softly, turning his attention to the hard tip of her breast, so very visible through her thin dress. "And just so you won't forget until I see you again..."

Before she realized what he meant to do, he bent and put his lips over the hard nipple and suddenly closed his teeth on it.

She gasped and pushed at him frantically, shocked and frightened by the intimacy.

He lifted his head, frowning, because her reaction puzzled him.

"My God," he breathed. "You don't surely think I meant to hurt you?"

"Di...didn't you?" she whispered shakily, all eyes.

He touched her gently, soothing the place his teeth had been, noticing that she flinched at even that light caress. "I'm sorry if I frightened you," he said tenderly. "Evidently you're used to gentler men altogether."

"Well, yes, I am," she faltered. It was true, too, but not in the way he meant it. She was still shivering from the force of what he'd made her feel. She'd never been so helpless. She couldn't have stopped him, no matter what he'd done to her, and now she realized what Winnie had been trying to tell her.

"I'm not a gentle lover," he said quietly, searching her eyes. "I've never had to be. My kind of woman can match my passion move for move, and it's always been rough and wild because I like it that way." He drew in a slow breath, and his hand flattened over her breast suddenly, in an almost protective gesture. "It never occurred to me before that some women might find that kind of ardor intimidating."

"I'm sorry," she said softly. "I didn't quite know what to expect."

Why in God's name he should feel guilty, he didn't know. But he did. He bent and kissed her with noticeable restraint, almost with tenderness. "Next time," he whispered at her lips, "I'll be a little less wild with you, and a hell of a lot gentler. The last thing I want is to make you afraid of me."

She searched his dark face with wonder. He seemed

as surprised by what they'd shared as she did. But he wasn't inexperienced. Shouldn't it have been routine to him to make love to a woman and experience those feelings? She wished she could ask him, but that would mean admitting her naïveté. And once he knew how innocent she really was, he'd never come near her again. He'd said so.

She tried to relax, to carry on the fiction of sophistication. But the blatant masculinity of his body against her made her uneasy.

"I'm not afraid," she said.

He moved his hand away from her breast and lightly touched her mouth, liking the way she lay so softly in his arms, her long hair draping around her shoulders, her eyes gentle and trusting now. She was a woman who needed tenderness, and he was angry with himself for the way he'd treated her. What had been natural with other women seemed out of place and crude with her. He remembered what he'd whispered to her, and winced now, wishing he could take it back.

"What is it?" she asked, having seen that change of expression.

"I said something pretty crude to you a few minutes ago," he said with quiet honesty. "I'm sorry. I suppose I'd forgotten that a woman with some experience can still be a lady, and deserves to be treated like one. The next time I make love to you, it won't be like this."

He moved her gently out of his arms while she was still absorbing the shock of what he'd said.

He went around the cab and helped her out, holding

her arm protectively as he escorted her onto the well-lit porch. He looked down at her and his eyes fell suddenly to her dress. He smiled ruefully.

"Good thing Winnie's not up," he murmured.

She followed his gaze and flushed. There was a very obvious dampness on her dress around the nipple that no engaged woman would mistake the reason for.

He cupped her face in his hands and held it up to his eyes, smiling indulgently at her. "Don't worry, no one will see it. Next time," he breathed, bending to her mouth with agonizing slowness, "we'll make sure the fabric is out of the way before I put my lips on you."

She gasped and he smiled against her mouth as he kissed it. His body went rigid instantly, drawing a shocked gasp from his own mouth.

"God, you excite me!" he said roughly, drawing back. "I'd better get out of here before I shock us both. I'll call in a day or so and we'll set a time for that trip to Hardin. By the way, you can tell your mother hen that I won't keep you out this late again."

"I will." She was holding his arms for support. It wasn't easy to let go. She didn't want to be away from him for a minute, much less two days. "Well, good night. I enjoyed the dinner and the concert."

"Not the movie?" he murmured dryly, smiling at her faint flush. His smile faded as he looked down into her eyes. "Never mind. I think I'm getting too old for careless passion." He touched her mouth with a long forefinger. "I would be tender with you," he said huskily. "I know enough to give you heaven. And when the time comes, I will. That's a promise."

Before she could get her breath or her wits back, he'd turned and was on his way back to the Jeep, his lean-hipped stride holding her eyes against her will. He was so good to look at, and what she felt with him was terrifying. She knew then, hopelessly, that she'd give him anything he asked for. She couldn't even run. The pull of attraction was too strong to fight. She watched him drive away without looking back and wondered sadly if this was how it would be when it was over, and he was going out of her life for good.

Gene knew she was still standing on the porch, but he didn't wave. He was teaming with new and confusing emotions that he really didn't want to explore too fully. His planned seduction was going sadly awry. His conscience was getting in the way.

Allison unlocked the door and went inside, half afraid that Winnie was going to see her. Impulsively she grabbed up a sweater from the clothes tree in the hall and slipped it on, pulling it over her breasts. And in the nick of time, too, because Winnie appeared in the hall as she was on the way to her room.

"About time, too," Winnie said worriedly. "Where have you been?"

Allison told her, making light of the date and raving over the symphony.

"So that's all it was," Winnie relaxed. She smiled ruefully. "I'm sorry. I know I'm overreacting. But he's so potent, Allie. So much a man…"

A sudden, horrible suspicion grew in the back of Allison's mind. "Is he?" she probed.

Winnie grimaced. "I guess you'd better know. I

dated Gene before Dwight cut him out. It was innocent; I never slept with him," she emphasized. "The thing is, I would have," she confessed miserably. "And he knew it. That's why I warned you. Gene takes what he wants, but he has nothing to give in return. You're playing a very dangerous game. I'm no Snow White, and I could have survived an affair with him—if I hadn't fallen so hopelessly in love with Dwight. But you're very innocent, Allie. I don't think you could live with yourself. Especially after your upbringing."

Allison. "I'm not sure I could, either," she confessed on a hard sigh. "He's…very potent."

"So I notice."

The amused drawl brought her eyes down and she noticed then that the sweater had fallen open. She went scarlet, wrapping it protectively over her breasts.

"Don't look so hunted," Winnie said gently. "I understand. A man like that is too hard to resist. You can't be blamed for being human. But to keep seeing him is asking for trouble."

"I know." Allison looked down at the floor. "I…think I'm falling in love."

Winnie bit her lower lip. "He can't help being the way he is. But he isn't a man who knows how to love. Or commit himself to a long-term relationship."

Allison looked up with haunted, sad eyes. "There's still a chance."

"And you're too hooked to listen to warnings, aren't you?" her friend replied gently. She hugged Allison to her with a sigh. "Try to keep your head, at least."

"I'll do that. Complications are the last thing I need."

"At least you know about precautions," Winnie sighed, smiling at Allison's flush. "Your training may come in handy before you're through. Okay, no more lectures. Go to bed. Is the wild man coming back?"

"Yes. Sometime in the middle of the week. He's taking me to see the Custer Battlefield. Then next week, we're going to the rodeo in Cody," she said.

Winnie just shook her head.

Allison changed into her nightgown, awed and frightened by the way it had been. Her first intimacy with a man, and she couldn't even admit it to him. She wondered if he'd have been different with her, had he known how naïve she was. Probably he'd have done what he swore at the beginning—he'd have left her strictly alone. He'd been honest about his opinion of innocence; that he wanted no part of it. She felt guilty about hiding hers, but she was falling in love. Even if he got angry at her later, she had to have a chance. He might fall in love with her, too, and then it would be all right.

Except that in the meantime he might seduce her, she thought worriedly. His ardor was unexpected and so was her helplessness. She'd never experienced those sensations, and they were addictive.

She tried to push it out of her mind when she went to bed. But she felt as if her body had scorched the sheets by morning. She'd never had such erotic dreams in all her life, and they were full of Gene.

Six

Gene was surprised by the force of his attraction to Allison. He'd meant to wait a few days before he saw her again, to give her time to miss him, to enhance her response to him. But he found himself thinking about her all too much. By the second day, the tables had suddenly turned on him and *he* was missing *her*.

He gunned the Jeep into the Manley driveway, smiling when he saw Allison out digging in Mrs. Manley's small flower garden near the porch steps. She was wearing Bermuda shorts and a pink tank top, her long black hair in a ponytail, and she looked charming. He cut off the engine and climbed out of the big vehicle, smoking a cigarette as he strode toward her, his bat-wing chaps making a leathery rustling sound as he walked.

"They've put you to work, I see," he drawled.

Allison flushed and smiled shyly, getting to her feet. She'd just been daydreaming about him, and here he was! "Hi!" she said, her whole face radiant with the greeting.

His heart jumped a little. "Hi, yourself," he murmured, moving closer. His eyes fell from her firm breasts down her narrow waist to softly flaring hips and long, elegant legs. She even had pretty feet, encased in brown leather thongs. "Nice legs," he murmured with a wicked glance.

"Thank you," she stammered. "Are you looking for Winnie and Mrs. Manley? They had to run to the store...."

"I came to see you, cupcake," he said softly, his wide-brimmed hat shadowing his eyes as they searched hers. "But I hardly dared hope I'd find you alone."

She felt her heart race. "Did you?" she whispered.

He tipped her chin up and bent his head unexpectedly, brushing his mouth with lazy expertise over her parted lips. "No, that won't do," he breathed, his voice deep and slow as he tossed the cigarette to the ground and reached for her. "Come close, little one."

He enveloped her in his muscular arms and drew her close as he bent again. This time the kiss was longer, harder, but so different from the way he'd kissed her two nights ago. This one was gentle, full of respect and warmth. She reacted to it with all her heart, sliding her arms under his and around his lean waist, loving the way his mouth played with hers and teased around it between kisses.

"Very nice," he mused when he lifted his head. It

was much better like this, gentle and sweet, so that she responded and didn't fight or draw away. He liked it when she wasn't frightened. "Dessert, in the middle of the day," he added, teasing. "You taste sweet."

She laughed softly, her hazel eyes adoring him. "I just ate a cinnamon bun."

"And that wasn't what I meant," he murmured. "Does tomorrow suit you to drive up to Hardin? We can leave about nine, if you like."

"Oh, yes," she said, already excited.

"Good. I'll make sure I'm free. Wear jeans and boots. There are rattlers in that area. I don't want you hurt."

Her smile widened. "I will," she promised, surprised and pleased that he was concerned about her. Being with him shot her through and through with pleasure.

He drew his forefinger down her nose. "Don't get sunstroke out here. What are you doing?"

"Weeding Mrs. Manley's flowers," she said. "I hate just sitting around. I hate soap operas and I can't do handicrafts. I like working."

The women he usually escorted liked to preen and put themselves on display. He scowled as he thought about it. Not one of them would like getting her hands dirty digging in a garden. His eyes slid over Allison's soft face and lingered there. His mother had been an enthusiastic gardener, too.

"Do you have a garden where you live?" he asked suddenly.

Her smile faded and she averted her eyes to the

spade she was using. "Yes, I had a vegetable garden," she said. "But it...was ruined."

"I'm sorry. I don't think Winnie's mother grows
vegetables."

"No, she's a flower enthusiast," Allison replied.
She looked up at him again, smiling as she studied
the way he looked in his working clothes, very lean
and lithe and Western. Very masculine, too, as he put
a match to the cigarette he'd just stuck in between his
thin lips. "You look like an ad for a Western vacation," she said involuntarily. "Very, very handsome."

He chuckled. "That's it, hit me in my weak spot."

She laughed, too. "You could have phoned. About
Hardin, I mean."

"I know." He touched her soft mouth lightly. "I
wanted to see you. Don't overdo. I'll pick you up at
nine."

"Okay," she said, her voice low and gentle.

He winked at her, but he didn't touch her again.
He pulled his hat down over one eye and strode back
to the Jeep. He didn't look back as he drove away.
She had a feeling that he never did, and it just vaguely
disturbed her. It was a reminder that he wasn't a committing man. And he was used to walking away from
women without looking back.

But by the time he picked her up the next morning,
she'd convinced herself that she was going to be the
one exception to his rule. He did at least seem to be
different with her since the other night, when she'd
drawn back from his overwhelming ardor. Maybe he
sensed her innocence and wasn't put off by it. She

laughed silently. More likely, he'd decided that roughness might put her off him, and he was soft pedaling his raging desire until he could coax her into satisfying it. She had to be realistic, but it was difficult when she was so vulnerable to him. That had to be mutual, though, she told herself. Otherwise, why would he have come all the way to the Manleys' to see her, when he could have phoned? She tingled with the delicious possibilities.

He was dressed in jeans and boots and a brown-and-white patterned Western shirt, the familiar Stetson cocked over one eye. Allison had dressed similarly, with a beige tank top under a blue-and-brown striped shirt. She laughed at the way they matched.

So did Gene. He helped her into the truck, jamming a Caterpillar bibbed cap down over her hair, which she'd pulled up in a soft bun. The cap came down to her eyebrows. "You can fix that. There's an adjustable strap in the back," he told her as he drove. "I figured you'd forget your hat."

She beamed. He was taking such good care of her. She looked at him, her heart overflowing with warm feelings. "Thanks," she said softly, and adjusted the plastic strip.

"I have to take care of my best girl," he said softly. The strange thing was that he meant it. She was the best girl he'd ever taken out. She wasn't demanding or petulant or sulky. She reminded him of bright summer sunshine, always cheerful.

She became radiant as she heard the words, blushing. It got worse when he reached out and tangled her fingers in his as he drove.

"Miss me?" he asked gently.

"Oh, yes," she said, not bothering with subterfuge.

He glanced at her, his eyes lingering on her rosy cheeks and soft, parted mouth before he forced his gaze back to his driving. "That goes double for me." His fingers clenched in hers. "You're good medicine, sunshine."

"Medicine?" she teased.

"Up in this part of the world, medicine means more than drugs. The Plains Indians used to 'make medicine' before battle, to protect them and help their spirits find the way to the hereafter. There was good medicine and bad, equally potent. They filled small rawhide bags with special talismans to protect their bodies from their enemies. Good medicine," he added, smiling as he glanced at her. "But I'd have hell stuffing you into a rawhide pouch."

She laughed. "I expect it would be uncomfortable, at that." Her eyes adored him. "Thank you for taking me to the battlefield. I've wanted to see it all my life."

"My pleasure. I don't think you'll be disappointed."

She wasn't. There was a museum and guided tours were available. She noticed that Gene avoided the groups of tourists as they meandered along the paved walkway up to the graves in their wrought-iron square and the tall monument on which was carved the names of the soldiers who died at the spot.

"We're standing on Crow land," he explained nodding down the ridge to the small stream that cut a deep ravine through the green grass. Beyond it was a large stand of trees and an even larger body of water. "Through there was the encampment. Several tribes of Sioux—Blackfoot, Sans Arc, Brule and Minneconjou—and a band of Cheyenne. In all, several thousand of them. This fenced area is where the last stand was made. Custer died here, so they say, along with his brother and brother-in-law and nephew. He was shot through the left breast and the temple."

"I read somewhere that he committed suicide."

He shook his head. "Unlikely. If you read his book, *My Life on the Plains*, you get a picture of a man who is definitely not the type for suicide. One authority on him thinks he was shot down in that ravine, through the left breast, and brought up here to the last stand position by his men. A bullet wound was found in his left temple. The Indians usually shot their enemies at close range to make sure they were dead. The Indians reported that after a buckskinned soldier was wounded in the ravine, the soldiers lost heart and seemed not to fight so hard. If it was Custer who got shot then, it would explain that near rout. His men were young and mostly inexperienced. Few of them had ever seen Indians on the warpath."

"I guess it would be scary," she said, looking up at him with fascination.

He lifted the cigarette he'd just lit to his mouth. "You don't know the half of it, cupcake. Plains Indians in full regalia were painted—faces, surely, and bodies. Even the horses were painted. Add to that the death cry they all yelled as they went into battle, and the eagle bone whistles they blew, and you've got a vision of death terrifying enough to make a seasoned trooper nervous."

"You said Sioux and Cheyenne; didn't the Crow fight the soldiers, too? We're standing on Crow land, you said," she added.

"It is. But the Crow saw the way of things, and allied themselves to the soldiers. The Cheyenne and Sioux were no more friends of the Crow than of the whites. Long before Sioux and Cheyenne came here, this was the land of the Absaroka—people of the fork-tailed bird. My God," he breathed, looking out over the rolling buttes and high ridges and vast stretch of horizon, "no wonder they fought so hard to keep it. Look. Virgin land, untouched, unpoisoned by civilization. God's country."

"Yes. It really is beautiful," she said.

The wind was blowing hard and he slid an arm around her, drawing her close. "Want to walk down to the ravine?" he asked.

"Could we?"

"Surely. There's a trail. Watch for snakes, now."

He led her down the deceptively long path to the ravine, stopping at each white cross that was supposed to mark the place where a man fell in battle. He seemed to know the names of all of them, and the history. He stopped for a long moment beside one marker.

"My great-great-uncle," he said, smiling at her expression. "Surprised? Now you know how I knew so much about the battle. His wife kept a journal, and I have it. The last entry was the night before he set out with Custer's 7th for the Little Bighorn. He probably kept a journal all the way here, too, but the Indian women scoured the battlefield after the fight, and took everything they thought they could use. Watches, pistols, clothing, even saddles and boots were carried off. The Indians threw away the soles of the boots and used the leather to make other things out of.''

"Tell me about your great-great-uncle," she said, and listened attentively while they walked back up from the steep banks of the ravine. He held her hand tightly, adding that an archaeological expedition had spent some time here only a year or so before, using teams of volunteers to help search with metal detectors and screened frames for artifacts from the battle after a fire had destroyed the brush that had covered it. She wasn't at all surprised to find that Gene Nelson had been among the volunteers.

He took her to a restaurant when they were through, at the Custer Battlefield Trading Post at Crow Agency. She wandered through the souvenir shop afterward, oohing and aahing over the exquisite beadwork on the crafts. She paused by a full-length warbonnet and sighed over a war lance. It was amazing to consider how terrifying these same things would have been to a woman only a hundred years before. Gene insisted on buying her a pair of beaded earrings for her pierced ears. On the way home, he explained the wearing of earrings by the various Plains tribes and how you could tell warriors of each tribe apart by their hairstyles and earrings.

"It's just fascinating," she said.

Gene glowed with pride. None of his dates had ever liked to hear him hold forth about the battle. Allison

not only listened, but she seemed to be really interested. He learned as they drove back that she was a
student of Indian cultures herself, and she seemed to
have a wealth of knowledge about the Mayans. He
listened to her on the way back, absorbing little-
known facts about that particular branch of Indian.

"You're good," he said when he drove up in front
of the Manley house just after dark. "Damned good.
Where did you learn all that?"

She smiled wistfully. "I just read a lot and kept
my ears open, I guess," she said, neglecting to add
that she'd climbed over Mayan temples where she and
her parents had been assigned. The smile faded as the
memories came back. "I had a good time, Gene. A
really good time. Thank you."

He drew her to him. "So did I." He searched her
eyes in the dim light from the dash. "We'll say our
good-nights here," he said softly, letting his eyes
drop to her mouth. "The way we kiss might shock
them."

As he whispered the words, his lips slowly parted
hers. They didn't take, they coaxed this time. Moist,
aching pressure teased her mouth open in a silence
that grew with strained breathing. He moved, so that
her head fell back against the seat, and his face followed hers, his mouth still teasing, provoking, tanta-
lizing until she was trembling.

"You set me on fire," he groaned as the need finally broke through. The pressure of the kiss pushed
her head hard into the back of the seat, and she felt
him shiver as his tongue slowly thrust past her teeth.
He groaned again, one lean hand sliding down her

throat to her breast under the shirt, over the thin tank top. "Stop wearing bras," he managed unsteadily. "They just get in my way."

She opened her mouth to speak, but no words came out. He was kissing her again, and this time his hand slid boldly right under the fabric. His thumb rubbed tenderly over her hard nipple, his moist palm cupping the firm underside of her breast. She moaned and he lifted his head.

"Satin and velvet," he said, his eyes glittery as they met hers. He deliberately pulled her tank top and bra out, so that he could look down at her taut, bare breast. "Yes," he said huskily, but without touching her this time. "You look as I knew you would. Pretty breasts. Tip-tilted and exquisitely pretty."

Her lips parted, but she was beyond shock. She shivered and actually arched toward him, so aroused that she wanted his mouth on her, there.

But he saw what she didn't—the curtains moving at the window. He released her reluctantly and lifted his head. "I can't touch you there," he said quietly. "Not now. We have an audience."

"Oh," she stammered, all at sea.

He lifted his invading hand back to her cheek and searched her eyes for a long moment. "We'll be good together," he said quietly. "You know it, too, don't you?"

She should tell him, she thought. She should... "Yes," she replied instead.

He nodded. "I won't rush you," he said. "But I won't wait a great deal longer, either. It's been too long for me."

She didn't know what to say. She shifted a little, still on fire in the aftermath of his ardor.

"Good night, sweet thing," he murmured, kissing her closed eyelids. "You're very special."

He drew back then and helped her out of the Jeep, keeping his arm around her as they walked back to the porch.

"Your guardian angel is hanging back," he mused, smiling down at her. "Is she giving up?"

Her heart leaped. "Sort of. She's engaged, you know."

He cocked an eyebrow. "So she is." He tapped her cheek. "I'll never be," he said suddenly. "You know that, don't you? I enjoy being with you, and physically, we burn each other up. But I won't lie and promise you happy ever after. I'm a confirmed bachelor."

Her heart didn't want to hear that. She forced a smile to her mouth. "Yes, I know."

He nodded slowly, searching her eyes. He couldn't let her get her hopes up. Marriage was definitely not on his agenda. He was still having hell coping with his past. And there was one very good reason why he didn't want to procreate. Bad genes could be passed on. He shifted. "Good girl. I'll pick you up tomorrow night and we'll go to the rodeo. I know I said next week, but I don't want to wait that long. Do you?"

She shook her head. "No. Not really," she confessed.

"Then I'll come for you at six." He nuzzled her face and kissed her softly. "Good night, pretty thing."

She smiled up at him a little wanly. "Good night. Thanks for the trip, and my earrings."

He twitched them, watching them dangle. "They suit you. See you tomorrow."

He was gone at once, without another kiss and still without looking back. She went into the house, smiling as Winnie came to meet her.

"We're just putting supper on the table," Winnie said. "Have fun?"

"Oh, yes. He knows a lot about the Custer battlefield, doesn't he?" she asked.

"Indeed he does. Did he bore you with it? Marie says he drives them crazy spouting history."

"But I love it!" Allison said, surprised. "Indian history is one of my hobbies. I found it fascinating."

Winnie's eyebrows went up. "My, my, imagine that." She grinned. "Way to go, tiger. You may land that feisty fish yet. Come on. I'll feed you."

The remark gave Allison hope, and she needed it. Her conscience was bothering her. She really should tell Gene the truth. If only she could be sure that he wouldn't turn around and walk away from her for good.

The next day, Allison decided that the best thing to wear to a rodeo—since her one pair of jeans was in the wash—was a full blue denim skirt with sporty pull-on pink sneakers and a pink T-shirt. But she wore a lightweight rose-patterned sweater with it, because she hadn't forgotten how cool it had been in Billings after dark. She pulled her hair into a ponytail and tied it with a pink scarf. Then she sat down to wait for

Gene, because she'd dressed two hours early for their
date. Every few minutes she involuntarily checked her
watch. The instrument was so much part of her uni-
form when she worked that she felt naked without it.
Despite the innovations in modern medicine, a watch
with a sweep second hand was about the most ad-
vanced equipment for pulse monitoring available in
the primitive areas where she and her parents had
worked.

Winnie's mother had been invited to a baby shower
for a friend's daughter, and Winnie was going out
with Dwight. They left just a few minutes before
Gene arrived. True to her word, Winnie didn't make
a single remark about the date. She just hugged Allison and smiled sympathetically. That was no surprise. Winnie was in love herself, so she certainly
understood how it felt.

Gene arrived exactly on time. He was dressed for
a casual evening, in jeans and hand-tooled black
leather boots with a blue patterned Western shirt and
a turquoise-and-silver bola. He wore a new black Stetson tonight with a moccasin headband, and he was
freshly shaved and showered.

He smiled down appreciatively at the way she
looked in her skirt and T-shirt with her silky black
hair in a ponytail. His body had given him no peace
for the past few days, going over and over the sweetness of Allison's response to him and the joy he'd
felt in her company. They shared so many common
interests that he actually enjoyed talking to her. Not
that the way they exploded when they touched was
any less potent. Not for worlds would he have ad-

mitted how much he'd looked forward to tonight. Looking at her made him feel good. Being with her was satisfying and sweet. And, unfortunately, addictive. He was going to have to do something about it; the sooner the better. She couldn't be staying much longer, and she was beginning to interfere with not only his work, but his sleep. He found himself thinking of her constantly, wanting to be with her. He was acting like a lovesick boy and he didn't want to disgrace himself by letting anyone know. The sooner he got her out of his system physically, the sooner he could get back to normal and deal with his worst problems.

The odd thing was that since Allison had been around, he hadn't worried so much about his parentage or that will that had changed his life. In fact, he was more at peace than he'd ever been. She gave him the first peace he'd had in weeks. Months. He felt as if there was no problem he couldn't overcome when he was with her. And that was disturbing. Really disturbing.

He pushed the thoughts to the back of his mind. "You look cute," he murmured dryly. "I like the T-shirt."

It read Women's Terrorism and Sewing Society. She'd found it in an out-of-the-way shop, and she loved it. She grinned up at him, her eyes warm in her oval face with its exquisite peaches-and-cream complexion. "It appealed to my sense of the ridiculous. Do you really like it?"

"I like the way you fill it out better," he said quietly, his eyes admiring her breasts and darkening with memory. "Is that skirt going to fall off without a belt?" he added, frowning at the way it fit in the waist—very loosely.

"I've lost a little weight in the past few weeks," she said noncommittally. "But it will stay up. I couldn't find my belt."

Of course not. It was still in Central America, along with most of her other belongings. That brought back vivid memories of how she'd left foreign surroundings, and how the media had followed her. Being seen in public could put her in jeopardy, but it was unlikely that Gene would introduce her to anybody from the press. She relaxed, shifting restlessly as she pushed the worries to the back of her mind.

He glanced around. "Where's Winnie?"

"Out with Dwight. Didn't you know?"

He laughed curtly, and without any real humor, his lean face full of mockery, his pale green eyes narrow and cool. "Dwight doesn't discuss his social life with me these days."

She moved closer to him, and because of the heels on his boots and the lack of them on her sneakers, she had to look up a lot farther than usual. He smelled of spicy cologne, a fragrance that made her pulse race almost as much as being close to him did. "He might, if you didn't make it so difficult for him," she said gently, and with a smile that took the sting out of the words.

He'd have thrown a punch at any man who dared say something like that to his face. But somehow it didn't offend him when Allison said it. One corner of his thin, disciplined mouth twitched and his eyes sparkled with faint amusement as he looked down at her.

"You standing in a ditch?" he asked unexpectedly. "Or did you get wet and shrink overnight?"

She laughed, her whole body on fire with life and love and his company. "I'm wearing sneakers."

"Is that it?" He looked down at her feet in pink tennis shoes. "Dainty little things," he mused.

"Nobody could ever describe *your* feet that way," she replied with a meaningful glance at his long boots.

"I throw away the boots and wear the shoe boxes," he agreed pleasantly. "Mrs. Manley isn't here, either?" he added, glancing around.

"She went to a baby shower."

He drew a slow breath, feeling a contentment he could hardly remember in his life stealing over him as he stared at her. "No lectures from your mother hen before she left with Dwight?"

She shook her head.

He chuckled. "She really has given up!"

"Yes." She searched his face quietly, loving every strong, lean line of it, its darkness, its masculinity. She could have stood looking at him all day.

His eyebrow jerked. Her delight was evident, and it made him bristle with pride. "We'd better go," he said after a minute.

"Yes."

But he didn't move, and neither did she. His eyes fell to her mouth, its pale pink owing nothing to lipstick. He caught her by the waist and drew her lazily against him, bending to brush his lips softly over hers in a delicate kiss that aroused but didn't satisfy. She tasted of mint and he smiled against her soft mouth, liking the hungry, instant response he got. Her arms moved up to hold him and he half lifted her against him in an embrace that made her think inexplicably of Christmas and mistletoe and falling snow, because she was warm and safe.

He wasn't thinking at all. The feel of her in his arms had stopped his mind dead. Everything was sensation now. Warm, soft breasts flattened against him, the floral scent of her body, the trembling eagerness of the soft lips parting under his rough mouth. His body stiffened as the first wave of desire hit him.

He forced himself to lift his head. He had to catch his breath, and she seemed similarly occupied. He searched her wide, stunned eyes for a long moment, until his heartbeat echoed in his ears like a throbbing drum.

Her face was beautiful. Her exquisite complexion was softly flushed, her lips were swollen and moist from the long, hard contact with his mouth. Wisps of black hair trailed around her rosy cheeks, and her hazel eyes looked totally helpless.

"It might be a good idea if we go, while we still have a choice," he murmured ruefully. He put her back on her feet and let her arms slide away from his neck. God, she was potent!

"Yes, it might," she agreed gently, equally affected and having a hard time dealing with it.

He waited while she locked the door and escorted her to the Jeep. "If you stick around long enough,

I'll buy a car," he murmured when they were driving off.

"I like the Jeep," she protested. "And it must come in handy on the ranch."

"It does," he had to agree. He glanced at her, frowning. So many secrets, he thought. She was mysterious, and he had a terrible secret of his own, about his real father. It would be better for both of them if he took her back to Winnie's and didn't see her again. But he couldn't seem to force himself to do that. Whatever happened, he had to have her, even if it was only one time. He knew instinctively that it would be different with her than it ever had been before; that it would be a kind of ecstasy he'd never known. He ached for her now. It was too late to stop it.

He'd smoked more lately than he had in his life. Occasionally he thought he'd die for a cigarette. This was one of those times. He lit one and opened the window, glancing at Allison.

"Do you mind?" he asked.

She leaned her head against the seat and studied his face warmly. "No."

"I'm trying to give it up. But sometimes things get to me."

"What things?" she asked gently.

"Life, Allison."

The sound of her name on his lips made her tingle. She liked the way he said it.

"It's been difficult for you, I know," she replied. "The important thing is that you'll get through it. Nothing lasts forever. Not even pain."

He scowled, darting a glance in her direction. "Don't bet on it," he replied.

Her eyes fell to his firm jaw, to the cut of his lips. She liked his profile. It was strong, like the man himself. "It's early days yet, though," she reminded him. "You can't expect to have your life torn apart and put back together overnight. I don't imagine that waiting comes easily to you."

He smiled in spite of himself. "No. It doesn't." He smoked quietly for a minute before he spoke again. "But in this case, I don't have a lot of choice. Are you impatient, Allison? Or do you find it easy to wait for the things you want?"

"I was always taught that patience was among the greatest virtues," she said simply. "But sometimes it's very difficult to stand back and not try to force things into place. Accepting things isn't much easier," she added, thinking of her parents.

He nodded. "I guess we're all human, aren't we, cupcake?" he asked quietly. "And there are times when it seems that we can't manage any control over our own destiny."

"You don't go to church, I guess," she asked softly.

He shook his head. "No." His face hardened. "I can't believe in a God who torments people."

"He doesn't," she said. "We do that to ourselves. He watches and helps when we ask Him, but I think we're somewhat responsible for our own destinies. When we have choices, we make them. Life takes care of the rest."

"And where does God enter into it?"

"He gave us free will," she said, smiling. "Otherwise, Eve would never have handed Adam that delicious, succulent juicy apple."

He burst out laughing. "Do tell?" he chuckled.

"Besides, there are other forces at work in the world. Balance means evil exists with good. Sometimes it's hard to win against the darker forces." Her eyes clouded. "That doesn't mean you quit trying. You just work harder."

"You sound like a minister we used to have," he mused without looking at her, which was a shame. The expression on her face would have fascinated him. "He wasn't a bad sort. I used to enjoy listening to him."

"What stopped you from going to services?" she asked, curious.

"I don't know," he shrugged. "I guess it was because it didn't seem to make any difference. Going to church didn't solve my problems."

"It doesn't solve them. It helps you cope with them," she said with a gentle smile. "Being religious doesn't automatically make you immune to hard times and hurt."

"That's what I discovered for myself. I expected miracles."

"Miracles are all around," she said. "They happen every day."

"Do they really?" he asked, unconvinced.

"Oh, yes." She could have told him that she was one. That she was alive was truly through divine intervention. She glanced out the window. "We aren't going through Shoshone Canyon again, are we?'' she asked, changing the subject delicately.

"No. I took you on a wide Western detour to show you the canyon and the tunnel. We're going northwest straight into Cody this time. Have you ever been to a rodeo?"

"Once or twice, down in Arizona. It's very dangerous, isn't it?"

"More than one cowboy has lost his life in a rodeo arena," he agreed. "All it takes is one small lapse of concentration, or carelessness. You can be gored by a bull, kicked by a horse, trampled, bitten, thrown so hard you break a bone... It's no game for city cowboys."

"Have any tried?" she asked, curious now.

He chuckled softly. "We had this guy from back East at one of the Cody rodeos last year," he began. "He'd been riding those mechanical bulls in bars and figured he was plenty good enough for a hick rodeo. He signed up and paid his entrance money. They put him up on one of the bulls we'd supplied. Old Scratch, by name." He grinned at her. "There he sat, waiting for the buzzer and for the gate to open, when the announcer gave Old Scratch's history and mentioned that in seventy-eight rides, not one cowboy had stayed on him until the horn sounded. The look on that dude's face was worth money."

"What happened?" she prompted.

"He and the bull parted company two seconds out of the chute. He broke his collarbone and one rib. Last I heard, he'd given up bull riding in favor of his old job—selling shoes at a department store back home.''

She gasped. ''Oh, the poor man!''

''Poor man, hell. Anybody who thinks riding almost a ton of bucking beef is a picnic ought to have his rear end busted. It's no game for shoe wranglers.''

She studied Gene's lean, hard face and let her eyes fall to his tall, fit body. ''Do you ride; in rodeos, I mean?'' she asked.

A smile touched his thin lips as he shot a quick glance her way. ''Do you think I'm too old, cupcake?''

She smiled back. ''No. I was just curious. I guess what you do at the ranch takes up most of your time.''

''It used to,'' he recalled bitterly. ''Until control of it passed to Dwight.''

''Dwight doesn't seem like the kind of person who'd take over everything,'' she said slowly, not wanting to offend him. ''I'm sure he was as upset as you were by what came out.''

He scowled. She hit nerves. He took a draw from his cigarette and abruptly put it out in the ashtray. ''I guess he was, at that,'' he said in a slow, even tone. ''He inherited the business side of the ranch, which he hates, and I wound up with the day-to-day operation of it, which I hate. I don't mind physical labor, you understand, but while I'm helping load cattle into trailers, Dwight's committing financial suicide with the accounts.''

''Haven't the two of you talked about that?'' she probed.

He tilted his hat across his brow. ''There's Cody

up ahead," he said, discouraging any further comment.

When he parked the Jeep and helped her out, it occurred to him that he'd told her more about himself than he'd shared with anyone in recent years. And in return, he'd learned nothing—not one damned thing—about her. He looked down at her steadily as they waited in line for tickets.

"You don't talk about yourself, do you?" he asked suddenly.

She lifted both eyebrows, startled by a question she hadn't expected. "Well, no, not a lot," she admitted.

"Is it deliberate?"

She shrugged. "I can't learn very much about other people if I spend my time talking about myself."

He tugged at her long ponytail mischievously. "I'll dig it out of you before I'm through."

"I'm shaking in my boots," she assured him.

"You aren't wearing boots."

"Picky, picky," she said, and laughed up at him. He was easily the most physically impressive man in the line, and the handsomest, to her at least.

"Well, hello, Gene," a soft, feminine voice drawled beside them, and a striking raven-haired beauty with flashing blue eyes attached on to his arm.

"Hello, Dale," he replied with a stiff nod.

"It's been months. Why haven't you called me?" the woman asked. She was dressed in rodeo clothes, satin and fringe with a white Stetson and matching boots. She was beautiful and younger than Allison by about three years.

"If I'd had anything to say, I would have," Gene

replied curtly, irritated by Dale's possessive manner and the blatant way she was leaning against him.

Dale's blue eyes glared at Allison. "Is she the reason?" she demanded, giving the older woman a hard appraisal. "She's hardly a beauty, is she?"

Gene took her arm roughly and moved her aside, his eyes as threatening as his cold tone. "Get lost. Now."

Dale tore away from him, glaring back. "You weren't so unfriendly once."

He gave her a mocking, icy smile. "I wasn't sober, either, was I?"

She all but gasped. Realizing that they were attracting attention, she turned and stormed off toward the back of the arena.

"I'm sorry about that," Gene told Allison, angry that she'd been embarrassed and hurt by Dale's harsh remarks.

Allison only nodded. So his conquests weren't in far-flung cities. She had a glimpse of how it might be if she married someone like him, and had to be constantly reminded of his wildness. Only a few months ago, the woman had said, and he was already resentful at having to see her again. Allison shuddered, thinking that she might have just seen herself in the future. She couldn't look up at Gene again. She was afraid of what she might give away.

But he sensed her discomfort. When they were seated in the bleachers waiting for the first event to start, he lit a cigarette and stared at her until she looked up.

"I'm sorry," he said curtly. His pale green eyes

searched her wan face quietly. "That couldn't have come at a worse time, could it?"

"She's very pretty," she voiced involuntarily.

"Yes. I was drunk and she was willing, and I thought that would be the end of it. But she's tenacious. I'd forgotten that she was entered in the barrel-racing competition tonight."

"Is she good?" Allison asked.

He glared at her. "In the saddle, or in bed?" he asked, taking the question at face value.

She averted her eyes. "In the saddle, of course."

His face hardened. "You take some getting used to," he said after a minute. "I always expect sarcasm from a woman. It's hard to acclimate to honesty."

"Maybe it's your choice of women that's at fault," she replied, trying to smile. Hearing him talk so casually about one of his conquests made her uncomfortable.

He had to admit that Allison wasn't like any of his other women. She appealed to a lot more than his senses. He scowled, because that bothered him. He drew on the cigarette as he stared toward the chutes. "Okay, honey, here we go," he said, nodding toward the announcer, who'd just started speaking.

It was the best rodeo Allison had ever seen. Gene knew most of the contestants and most of the livestock, so he pointed out the strongest riders in each competition and the worst bulls and broncs.

"Now that son of a mustang leaped flat-footed into the back seat of a convertible on a neighboring ranch," he informed her as one of the worst bareback broncs trotted away after unseating his would-be rider. "He doesn't belong to us, and I'm glad. He's a really bad customer. All but unridable and bad-tempered to boot. I've been kicked by him a time or two myself."

"You said you didn't ride," she remarked.

"Not often," he corrected. "Now and again when I've had a beer too many, I get the old urge to try to break my neck in the arena," he chuckled.

That didn't sound encouraging, either, as if he liked to go on binges. Allison knew so little about men and their habits. She really had led a sheltered life.

"Look, here comes one of ours," he said, nudging her. "That's Rocky Road. He can outbuck most of the others hands down."

Sure enough, the bronc unseated his rider in jig time and sashayed off without a care in the world. The cowboy he'd unseated slammed his hat down in the dirt and jumped on it repeatedly while the audience laughed at the unexpected entertainment.

Allison laughed with him. She really couldn't help it.

"Oh, the poor man," she choked.

"You pay your money and take your chances," he said without much real sympathy. "It happens to all of us. The name of the game is to keep down the number of winners. A rodeo exists to make money, not to give it away, you know."

"I guess I didn't think. But I still feel sorry for the men who lose."

"So do I, if you want to know."

The next man stayed on and Allison thought he'd done extremely well, but he didn't score at all.

"He didn't get thrown!" Allison protested on the man's behalf.

"The horse didn't buck enough, honey," Gene explained patiently, and then went on to describe how a cowboy had to rake his spurs from the horse's neck down to his flanks on each leap, how he had to keep one hand free at all times, and that he was judged on much more than just staying on the horse's back.

"It's so complicated." She shook her head.

"That's the name of the game," he replied. He smiled down at her. "If you watch rodeo enough, you'll get the hang of seeing how it's judged. That's an art in itself."

She smiled back at him, tingling from head to toe at the warm, intimate look in his eyes before they averted back to the action down in the arena. She couldn't remember when she'd felt happier or more alive. Especially when Gene appropriated her hand and clasped it warmly in his while they watched the rest of the competition.

The last of the bareback bronc riding finished, with the winner and second and third places announced. Then came barrel racing, and the woman named Dale was competing. Allison noticed that Gene didn't applaud or pay much attention to the pretty young woman in the arena. He didn't even react when his ex-lover won the race. Dale Branigan, they announced, and Allison stared down at the younger woman with envy. She was pretty and young and full of the joy of life as she reacted to her win by jumping in the air and giving out a loud, laughing yell. So that was the kind of woman who attracted the taciturn man

at her side: young, aggressive, eager for intimacy, and
fancy-free. She didn't really have much of a chance.
That might be a good thing, considering how he
seemed to treat women he'd slept with. She felt suddenly sad. She was daydreaming, and it was no good.
He might be wonderful to kiss, and delightful as a
companion, but it was all just means to an end, she
was sure of it. The thought depressed her terribly,
although Gene didn't seem to notice. He was quiet
after the barrel racing.

He felt Allison's gaze, but he didn't meet it. Seeing
Dale again had disturbed him. He remembered very
little of the night he'd spent with her, and now he was
ashamed of his part in it. The old Gene wouldn't have
had any qualms at spending the night in the arms of
a pretty, willing woman. But since he'd been taking
Allison places, the ease of his old conquest disturbed
him. He couldn't sort out the confused feelings he
was entertaining for Allison, or the guilt she aroused
in him sometimes. She seemed to look for the best in
everyone and everything, as if she wouldn't even admit the existence of evil in people. She was caring
and kind and gentle, and sensuous in a strange, re-
served way. He was surprised at her inhibitions when
he kissed and held her intimately, and he wondered
why her own conquests hadn't taught her more. Perhaps she'd been sleeping with the wrong men. He
thought about sleeping with her himself, and his body
vibrated with excitement. It would be like having a
virgin, he thought, and his heartbeat increased
fiercely. He didn't dare look at her until he got himself under control again.

Unaware of his thoughts, Allison concentrated on the arena. But there seemed to be a distance between Gene and herself, and she didn't understand why.

In no time, the competition was over, the prizes awarded, and it was time to go home. Allison followed Gene down from the bleachers, noting his dark scowl as he saw Dale coming toward them with her award.

"Going to congratulate me?" she asked Gene, apparently having recovered from her bad humor, because she was smiling seductively.

"Sure. Congratulations." He slid an arm around Allison's shoulders and drew her close, glancing down at her possessively. "We thought you were great, didn't we, cupcake?" he added, his voice low and caressing for Allison.

She smiled with difficulty, going along with the pretense. "Yes." She looked at the younger woman with kind eyes. "You were very good."

Dale shifted restlessly under that warm, easy smile, which showed no trace of antagonism or hostility. She didn't know how to react to a woman who didn't behave like a spitting cat. "Thanks," she said uneasily. "Going to the dance?" she added.

"We might," he said.

"Going to introduce me?" she persisted, nodding toward Allison.

"This is Allison Hathoway," he said, glancing down at her. "She's an old friend of Winnie's. You know Winnie—she's engaged to Dwight."

"I know her. Nice to meet you. I'm Dale Branigan." She extended a hand and shook Allison's firmly, her blue eyes unwavering. "Are you just visiting?"

Allison nodded. "For another week or so," she said, hating to put into words how little time she had left. But she couldn't impose much longer on the Manleys, and she had to go to Arizona and finish tying up the loose ends of her parents' lives. It was a task she didn't anticipate with pleasure.

Gene stiffened. He hadn't realized how soon she planned to leave. It disturbed him to think of her going away, and he didn't understand why.

Allison felt the sudden stiffening and looked up at Gene just as he glanced down at her. The tension exploded between them so that it was almost visible. Dale said something and left and neither of them noticed her departure. Allison's lips parted under the force of the shared look, the impact like lightning striking. Her heart raced.

"Do you want to go to a dance with me?" he asked huskily, his body suddenly on fire. "It would mean going home very, very late."

"Yes." She spoke without hesitation. She didn't want to go home yet; she didn't want to say goodnight to him. She wasn't considering the dangers of being seen in public or giving the media any clues to her whereabouts. She wanted to be held in his arms, for as long as possible. She was too much in love to care about the consequences anymore.

Gene was feeling the same thing. His world had just narrowed to the woman beside him. "All right," he said curtly. "To hell with the consequences. Come on."

Seven

The dance that followed the rodeo was in a local bar and grill, and nothing fancy by city standards. It was very casual, with men and women both in jeans and Western hats, in what looked like a converted barn.

Gene ordered two beers, ignoring Allison's grimace, and seated them at a small round table near the dance floor. There was a live band and no shortage of dancers. The place was packed with celebrators from the rodeo.

"But..." she protested when Gene put the mug of foamy beer in front of her.

"Taste it first," he coaxed gently. "It won't hurt you. One beer isn't going to do much damage, and I've ordered some sandwiches to go with it. Okay?"

She sighed, still reluctant.

He leaned toward her, one lean forefinger tracing

patterns on the back of her hand while his eyes held hers. "I like beer. I'll taste of it when we leave here." His gaze fell to her mouth. "If you taste of it, too, it won't bother you when we make love."

Her lips parted and her heart jumped. "Tonight?" she stammered, because he looked as if he meant business this time.

"Tonight, Allison," he said huskily. He caught her eyes again and held them, his whole body throbbing with anticipation. She was staring back at him just as intently and he felt his body react fiercely. He leaned closer, his lips almost touching hers as he spoke. "There's a line cabin between here and the house," he breathed. He caught her chin and tilted it gently so that his thin lips could brush lightly over hers in a whisper of rough persuasion. "I promise you, I won't be rough. It will be exactly the way you want it, all the way."

She tried to speak, but his teeth closed on her lower lip, tugging, and before she could get a word out, the moist warmth of his mouth buried itself in hers. She was so sweet. He could hardly breathe for his need of her. He hadn't meant to let it go this far, but once he felt her mouth under his, he couldn't stop.

He wasn't the only one. Allison shivered with reaction. Her mouth answered his, blind to where they were, deaf to the people and music around them, hopelessly lost in him. Nothing mattered except being in his arms. She'd been alone so long, been through so much. Surely she could be given this one, sweet night! To lie in the arms of the man she loved and be cherished, just one time. The temptation was overwhelming. And he'd said he'd be gentle. That had to mean he cared. Hadn't he told her at the beginning that he was always rough because that was the way he liked it—and now here he was putting her wants before his. He had to care, a little.

When he lifted his head, they were both breathing roughly. He had to force himself to draw away. With a jerky movement, he reached for his mug of beer and all but drained it.

"I didn't mean to do that, yet," he said unsteadily. He stared at her solemnly, his eyes lingering on her delicately flushed face with its exquisite complexion. Her eyes were misty, a little dazed, and her mouth was swollen and parted from the long, hard kiss. Just the sight of her knocked the breath out of him.

"It's all right," she said huskily.

He averted his gaze and found himself looking at Dale, who was dancing stiffly with a plain, lanky man wearing a red shirt. She gave him a pouting, accusing look before she turned her attention back to her partner.

Allison followed the cold stare of his eyes. "She's very pretty," she remarked quietly.

He turned, his gaze glittering. "Yes. But she wanted more than I could give her."

Was she like that, too, Allison wondered, wanting more than he had to give? It didn't seem to matter. She was too hopelessly in love with him to let it matter tonight. Soon she'd be alone again, for the rest of her life. Just this one night, she prayed silently. And then the thought bored into her mind—be careful what you ask for...you might get it.

She quickly lowered her gaze to her own beer. She cupped her hands around the frosty mug and lifted it to her lips, making a face when she tasted it.

She looked over at Gene. They came from different worlds. He wouldn't understand her hang-ups any more than she could understand his lack of scruples with women. She'd told a lie and now it was catching up with her. Despite the fact that he'd opened up to her, that they were getting along well together, she was still afraid to tell him the truth about herself. But would it matter—if he were gentle? She flushed.

Her eyes searched his stern expression. There was a different man that he kept hidden from the world. She caught glimpses of him from time to time, behind the sarcasm and tough facade. She wanted a glimpse of the lonely, wounded man he was hiding.

A sudden cry split the noise of people and music, and suddenly everything around them abruptly stopped.

"What is it?" Allison asked, frowning as she looked toward the bar.

He turned in his seat and stood. "Oh, boy," he murmured. "Somebody broke a beer bottle and cut his hand half off. Dale's new beau, Ben, no less."

Allison got up without a word and went to the hurt man. She smiled at Dale and then at the cowboy, who was holding his hand and shivering with pain while Dale tried ineffectually to stem the flow of blood.

"Let me," she said gently, taking the cloth from Dale's shaking hands. "I know what to do."

She did, too. Gene watched her with fascination, remembering how efficiently she'd patched him up.

He wondered where and why she'd gotten her first-aid training. She was good at it, calm and collected and quietly reassuring. Even Dale relaxed, color coming back into her white face.

"That should do it," she said after a few minutes of applied pressure. "Fortunately it was a vein and not an artery. But it will need stitches," she added gently, cleaning her hands with a basin and cloth the bartender had provided after she'd put a temporary bandage over the cut. "Can you drive him to the hospital?"

"Yes," Dale said. She hesitated. "Thanks."

"That goes double for me," the cowboy said with a quiet smile of his own, although he was still in a lot of pain. "I could have bled to death."

"Not likely, but you're welcome. Good night."

They left, and Allison noticed that Dale gave Gene a long, hurting look even as she went out the door with her wounded cowboy. Poor thing, she thought miserably. Maybe she'd look like that one day, when Gene didn't want her anymore.

Without sparing her a glance, Gene led Allison out onto the dance floor. "Full of surprises, aren't you?" he mused. "Where did you learn so much about first aid?"

"I had a good teacher," she said noncommittally, smiling up at him.

He scowled down at her. "I can't dig anything out of you, can I?" he asked quietly. "You're very mysterious, cupcake."

"There's nothing out of the ordinary about me," she laughed. "I'm just a working girl."

"When are you leaving the Manleys'?" he asked suddenly.

She lowered her eyes to his broad chest. "Next week. I don't want to, but I need to," she said. "I've got a lot to do."

"Where?"

"In Arizona," she said.

"Is that where you work?"

She hesitated. "I guess it's where I'll be working now," she replied. She didn't want to think about it. Life was suddenly very complicated, and the worst of it was going to be leaving here and not seeing Gene Nelson again.

He sighed half angrily. One lean arm pulled her closer and he turned her sharply to the music, so that his powerful leg insinuated itself intimately close to hers.

She stiffened a little and he slowed, pausing to look down at her.

"Don't fight it," he said huskily. "Life's too short as it is, and what we've got together is magic." And with that, he caught both her arms and eased them under his and around him while his circled her, bringing her totally against him.

"Gene," she protested weakly.

"This is the way everyone else is doing it, if you want to look around us. Put your cheek on my chest and give in."

She knew it was suicide, but she couldn't help her own weakness. She moved close to him with a long sigh and laid her cheek against his hard chest. Under his blue patterned shirt she could feel the warmth of his body and the rough beat of his heart. He smelled of soap and cologne and starch, and the slow caress of his hands on her back was drugging.

They moved lazily around the floor as the lights dimmed and the music became sultry. Everyone was relaxed now, a little high from the beer and revelry, and when Gene's hands slid down to her lower spine and pulled her intimately to him, she didn't protest.

His lean, fit body began to react to that closeness almost at once. He felt himself going rigid against her, but he didn't try to shield her from it. It was too late, anyway.

He lifted his head and looked down into her eyes while they danced. She looked a little nervous and uncertain, but she wasn't protesting.

His eyes fell to her breasts, lingering on them. With a low murmur, he drew his hands up her back to her ribcage and slowly, torturously moved her toward him so that her breasts brushed sensuously against his hard chest, making the tips suddenly hard and swollen. He could feel them even through the fabric, and when she trembled, he felt that, too.

His eyes lifted to hers, and held them as his hands moved again, down, down, until they reached her hips. He lifted her gently and her thighs brushed his, hard.

Her breath caught. She flushed, because even an innocent couldn't mistake what he was feeling and what he wanted now. But the worst of it was that she wanted it just as much. She was caught in a sensual daze and her body ached. She wanted him to kiss her.

She wanted his hands on her body to soothe the burning ache he'd created. She wanted…him.

He stopped dancing and stood with her in the middle of the dance floor, his pale eyes glittery as they searched hers. "I want to take you out of here," he said huskily. "I can't stand much more of this."

"Yes," she whispered. She knew what he was saying, and part of her was ashamed and frightened and reluctant. But she cared too much to refuse him.

"All right." He let her move slowly away from him, but he didn't let her go. "I need a minute, cupcake," he said softly. He pulled her back into his arms, but so that their legs didn't touch. He drew in deep breaths until he could get his body back in control so that what he felt wouldn't be on public display. Then, gently, he led her off the dance floor and out the door to the Jeep, ignoring the sandwiches he'd already paid for that had just been placed on their table. Food was the very last thing on his mind right now.

"Did you enjoy the rodeo?" he asked on the way home. He hadn't touched her or said anything vaguely romantic since they'd left the bar. He was smoking like a furnace, but that could mean anything. Allison was still in a daze, and her body was on fire to be held close to his. But she tried to keep that to herself.

"I enjoyed it very much," she said. "I never realized the events were so complicated."

"It helps when you know a bit about it," he said. He was nervous. Imagine that, he thought with graveyard humor, and with his reputation. But Allison wasn't like other women he'd made love to. She was

very, very special, and he wanted this to be like no
other time for her. He wanted to give her everything.

He pulled off the main road and drove toward the
ranch, but there was a dirt track that led into a grove
of trees by the creek, and he took that one instead of
the ranch road that led home.

Allison felt herself tensing, because she knew instinctively what was in that grove of trees down the
road. But she didn't say a word. She'd committed
herself back in Cody. It would be cowardly and cruel
to back down now. Of course, that was only an excuse
to appease her conscience, and she knew it. She
looked at the man beside her and knew that she'd do
anything he asked of her. No one had ever been so
gentle and kind to her, no man had ever made her
feel so special. He'd rescued her from a kind of limbo
that she'd been in ever since her parents death.

"The line cabin is down there," he said, trying not
to show how desperately he needed her or how nervous he was. "It's old. Probably the oldest building
still in use on the place. The men stay here during the
winter when they have to keep up with the outlying
herds."

"I see."

He pulled up in front of a small, darkened cabin
that looked like something out of a history journal
and cut the engine and the lights. "It doesn't look
like much, but it's pretty well kept."

He got out and helped her out, then led her up the
porch to the front door and inside. She felt oddly
light-headed, probably, she thought dizzily, the result
of the beer and no food.

"See, we even have electricity," he mused, turning on a small lamp.

The cabin was only one room, with a small kitchen, a fireplace and two chairs, and a neatly made bed with a blue-beige-and-red patterned quilted coverlet over it. Just the thing, Allison thought, for a cowboy on his own in the winter.

"The bed linen is washed weekly, even if nobody stays here, and we keep a supply of food in the kitchen," he told her. He turned, his gaze slow and warm on her face as he took off his Stetson and tossed it onto a chair. She looked so young, he thought, watching her. So sweet and vulnerable and hungry for him. His heart raced.

Without another word, he unfastened his bola and unsnapped the buttons down the front of his shirt with a dark, lean hand.

Her breath caught in her throat as he pulled the shirt out of his jeans and opened it. His chest was darkly tanned and thick with curling black hair. He moved toward her with a faintly arrogant expression, as if he knew how exciting and sensuous he was without the trembling of her body and the sudden parting of her lips to tell him.

He caught her cool hands and brought them under the lapels of the open shirt, pressing them palm down on his warm, rough chest. The sensation was incredible. He shivered. "Feel me," he said huskily, moving her hands around. He drew her to him and bent to her lips, pausing just above them to tease them, torment them, while he let her hands learn the contours of his torso. It was sheer heaven, the feel of those soft, warm fingers on his taut body. He felt himself going rigid all at once and didn't even try to hold back.

"Allison," he groaned as he bent to her mouth. "Oh, God, I've never wanted anyone so much!"

The wording weakened her, because she knew how he felt. Odd, with his reputation that he could be so vulnerable to an innocent like her. Of course, she thought uneasily, he didn't know she was innocent. His hands were moving over her back and she hesitated for just one second with maidenly fear of the unknown. Then she relaxed as the kiss began to work on her, his exploring lips making her mouth soft and eager for its moist, warm touch.

All at once, the wanting broke through his control. His tongue shot into the dark softness of her mouth in a rhythm that was staggeringly sensual and arousing. She gasped in shocked pleasure. But there was more to come.

His lean hands caught the backs of her thighs and lifted her up to his aroused body in a sharp, quick rhythm that made her knees go weak and shaky. Sensations of hot pleasure rippled through her lower belly like the tide itself. She shuddered all over and grabbed his arms to keep from toppling over at the feverish need she felt. She cried out under his mouth, and he made a deep, satisfied sound in his throat.

He bent, lifting her totally against him, her feet dangling as his hands suddenly brought his hard thighs between her legs in the full skirt and pressed her intimately to him.

She moaned harshly, clinging, almost in tears from

the sudden fury of her desire of him. She knew in the back of her mind that this was wrong, that she was letting him go too far, but she was helpless from the hot surge of passion he'd kindled in her. She'd never known such pleasure.

Her mouth answered his, giving him back the deep kiss as hungrily as he offered it. He felt his own body begin to tremble and he knew there was no way he could stop now. It had gone too far.

He fell onto the bed with her, shivering with need, his hands trembling as they slipped her out of her sweater and T-shirt and the filmy bra she wore under them. He didn't stop there, either. While he was at it, he unsnapped the skirt and kissed his way down to her thighs while he smoothed the rest of her clothing down her body and tossed it aside with her shoes.

She lay nude under the slow, insistent brush of his hard mouth. His hands explored while his mouth learned every soft curve of her in a silence that grew hotter with her soft cries of pleasure and the helpless movements of her body on the springy mattress.

He lifted his head while his fingers brushed expertly over the hard crests of her breasts and he looked into her eyes with pure masculine need. She was shivering, her eyes wide and glazed, her lips parted under hopelessly gasping breaths. Her long legs were moving helplessly on the bed in little jerky motions. Yes, he thought feverishly, and he touched her gently where she was most a woman, deliberately adding to her helplessness as shocks of pleasure lifted her hips and closed her eyes.

He didn't question why she should be so easily and

quickly aroused, or why her eyes opened in something like faint shock when he threw off his shirt and boots and socks and started unzipping his jeans with quick, economical movements. He didn't question why she lifted up suddenly on her elbows and gasped when he turned, his blatant arousal the crowning glory of a body that some women had called perfection itself. His mind was buried in the desire for her that had made him shuddering at just the sight of that creamy pink body with its firm, soft breasts and exquisite figure, lying there waiting for him, trembling.

He straddled her hips arrogantly, watching her watch him with wide, almost frightened eyes.

"You can take me, if that's what you're frightened of," he said gently, levering down so that his body slowly overwhelmed hers, his elbows catching his weight. "A woman's body is a miracle," he whispered at her lips. "Elastic and soft and vibrant with life." His mouth brushed hers in tender little contacts that aroused like wildfire while his hands smoothed down her body, his thumbs hard on her belly, rough, making some unbelievable sensations kindle with each long pass of his hands. She shivered under his warm mouth, her nudity and his maleness almost forgotten until his knee began to ease between her long legs.

"Shhh," he whispered when she tensed. "Don't do that. I want you just as badly, but if you tense up, it's going to hurt."

She swallowed. It would hurt anyway, but it was too late to tell him that, because his hips were already probing delicately at hers.

He kissed her face with trembling, aching tenderness, while his lean hands gently positioned her hips. "One, long, sweet joining," he whispered into her open mouth. "That's what I want first, before I even begin to love you." His thumbs pressed into her belly again, making her shiver. He smiled tenderly against her lips. "Now lift up against me, very, very slowly," he whispered. He lifted his eyes to watch. He'd never wanted to watch before, but this was like no other time in his life. Her eyes were wide, almost frightened. "Shhh," he breathed, achingly tender as he began the slow, downward movement of his body. "Shhh. Be one with me, now," he whispered. She tensed and he smiled, sliding one hand between them to gently caress her flat belly. "Yes, just relax and let it happen. Don't close your eyes," he said huskily. "Watch me. Let me watch you. I want...to see you...take me!"

His teeth ground together and Allison was so shocked by what he was saying and doing that she forgot to be afraid. His powerful body was tanned all over, except for that pale strip across his lean hips, and she saw his eyes dilate, his teeth clench, his face contort with wonder. She could feel the shudder that went through him, she could actually see him lose control.

It was what made it bearable when he suddenly cried out and pushed into her body with helpless, driving urgency. The pain was scalding, like being torn with a hot knife, and she both stiffened and dug her fingers into his arms, weeping suddenly as he hurt her.

But she was too ready for him for it to last long. Gene felt the barrier give, somewhere in the back of his mind, although it didn't register through the blinding throb of pleasure that ran down his backbone and sent him wild in her arms. He buffeted her with a total, absolute loss of control, borne of too many months of abstinence and his raging hunger for her. A loaded gun wouldn't have stopped him.

Allison heard the springs rocking, felt the breeze through the open window, and wept silently for her lack of resistance. He was going to hate her. He couldn't not know what she was, now.

Seconds later, he stiffened and cried out, and Allison watched his corded torso lift as his hips enforced their mastery of her, watched his face contort in the unmistakable mask of fulfillment. His voice throbbed hoarsely as he cried her name once, twice, and then like a prayer, his body convulsed in a red fever of blinding ecstasy.

It hadn't hurt as much as she thought it would. He was lying on her heavily now, his body drenched in sweat, his mouth against her bare shoulder. Still flushing from what she'd seen, she stroked his damp, black hair absently, her eyes wide and shocked as she stared at the rough wood of the ceiling. Despite everything it was so sweet to lie and hold him like this, so close that they were still one person. The embarrassment and pain and shame would follow, she knew, and would be almost unbearable. But for these few seconds, he was helpless and in need of comfort, and she held him to her with tender generosity, her eyes closing as she whispered her love for him silently, without a sound.

Gene got his breath back and lifted his head to look at Allison. Her eyes opened slowly and she blushed. There was something in those soft hazel eyes that hurt him. He'd failed her all the way around.

He accepted the knowledge with shame and a kind of helpless pleasure as his eyes slid down to her breasts, still hard-tipped because he hadn't satisfied her. He would have been more than willing to do that, because she'd given him heaven. But it would be too soon for her, after the ordeal of her first time. First time. He shivered. A virgin. He was her first man.

The thought humbled him. He bent and started to kiss her soft mouth, but she turned her head, and then he saw it. The shame. The fear. He took a sharp breath and rolled away from her, standing up to dress quietly, with cold efficiency. It had never been like that, he thought bitterly; it had never been so urgent that he couldn't wait for his partner. He couldn't even blame the beer, because he hadn't had that much. And he knew damned well he hadn't satisfied Allison. There hadn't been time. Besides that, he thought, horrified as he turned to look at her, she'd been unnaturally tight and afraid and now he knew that he must have hurt her terribly. They said no man could tell, but even without glancing at that faint stain on the coverlet, he knew. Somehow, he thought he'd known from the beginning. And if his own guilt was enough, she wouldn't even look at him. She made him feel like less than a man.

He looked away while she put on her own clothes

with trembling hands. When he turned again, a smoking cigarette in his hands, she was sitting on the edge of the bed with her hands folded on her thighs, her eyes downcast, her thin body trembling.

The most beautiful experience of his life, and he'd cost her not only her chastity but any pleasure she might have had, all because he'd been selfish. She looked as if what she'd done was some unforgivable sin to boot. Her downcast, defeated expression made him hurt. His guilt and self-contempt spurred his temper, and he exploded with rage.

He reached out and grabbed her arms, jerking her roughly to her feet. "Damn you," he said icily, shaking her none too gently. His blazing eyes made her flinch. "You lied to me! You told me you were experienced, when all the time you were a virgin!"

She all but cringed, closing her eyes. Neither of them saw or heard the shadowy figure on horseback who'd heard that furious accusation. The rider moved a little closer and spotted them through the window, a sarcastic smile on his mouth. He didn't hesitate. He abruptly turned his mount and stealthily rode away.

"Why did you do it?" Gene was demanding.

"I wanted to get to know you," she said dully.

"Well, you did, didn't you?" he asked with deliberate cruelty, and a meaningful glance at the stain on the coverlet.

Her eyes dropped on a hurting moan. Tears were rolling down her cheeks without a sound. She stared at his throat, watching the pulse throb there. She deserved the anger, so she didn't fight it. He was right. She'd lied and let him think she was experienced and because of it, he hadn't felt any need to hold back physically. Now he'd seduced her and she only had herself to blame. Worse than that, she hadn't taken any precautions or asked him to. One time might not be anything to worry about, of course, but there were no guarantees. And she still had to live with her guilt and shame, with her conscience.

He let go of her abruptly, savagely ashamed of his own uncharacteristic behavior. He didn't think he'd ever be able to look at her again without hating himself.

Allison, of course, didn't realize that his anger was directed at himself, not at her. She thought he surely must hate her now, and she couldn't bear to meet his eyes.

He noticed, with bitter pain. "We'd better go," he said coldly.

He turned out the light and jerked open the door, helping her inside the Jeep with icy courtesy before he went back to lock the cabin again. He got into the Jeep without a single word, and that was how he drove home.

When he pulled up at the Manleys' house, she got out without assistance, clutching her purse, and she didn't say anything or look back as she went up onto the porch. Shades of Gene Nelson himself, she thought with almost hysterical humor. Wasn't he the one who never looked back?

But apparently he wasn't going to let her get away with it that easily. He went with her, staying her hand as she started to unlock the door.

"Are you all right?" he asked tersely, forcing the words out.

"Yes." She didn't look up. Her soul was tarnished.

He took off his Stetson and ran a hand through his hair. "Allison," he began hesitantly. "What I said back there…"

"It doesn't matter," she replied numbly. "I have to go in now. I'm sorry about…about what happened. I've never had alcohol before."

"And that was why?" he asked with a mocking laugh. "You were drunk?" Deny it, he was thinking. For God's sake, tell me it was because you loved me!

But the silent plea passed into the night. She unlocked the door. "Goodbye, Gene," she said gently, even now unable to blame him for something she'd encouraged to happen.

"Isn't that a little premature?" he asked hesitantly.

"I'll be leaving in the morning," she said without looking at him. "You won't have to worry that I'll…be like Dale and hound you…" Her voice broke and she got inside fast, closing and locking the door behind her.

Gene stood staring at the closed door for a long moment. He felt empty and alone and deeply ashamed. What had possessed him to attack her, as if the whole thing was her fault? She was a gentle woman, with a soft heart and a heavy conscience, and it bothered him that she'd looked so torn when he let her go. She talked about religion a lot and church, and he wondered if she believed sleeping around was a mortal sin. It amazed him that he hadn't seen through the act, that he'd really believed she was experienced, when everything pointed the other way. If he'd kept his head, he'd have known in time that she was innocent, and he could have stopped. But he didn't know, and he hadn't been rational enough to control his raging desire. A desire that he still felt, to a frightening degree. Allison. He felt her loss to his very soul. In a few days she'd become an integral part of his life, his thoughts. He wasn't sure if he could go on living when she left Pryor. Could half a man live?

He turned and went back to the Jeep, cursing himself all the way. She'd leave and he'd never have the opportunity to apologize. Not that she was completely blameless, he told himself. It hadn't been all his fault. But what had motivated her? Had it been desire? Loneliness? Curiosity? Or had there been some feeling in her for him? She was a virgin and she'd given herself. Would she really have done that, being the kind of person she was, unless she cared deeply? His heart leaped at the thought of Allison loving him.

Of course, she was twenty-five and modern, he reminded himself grimly. Maybe she was just tired of being a virgin. He didn't like to consider that last possibility. And even if she had begun to care about him, she surely wouldn't now. His cruelty would have shown her how fruitless that would be. He climbed into the Jeep and lit another cigarette before he started the engine and pulled out of the yard. This time he stopped the car, and he looked back. It was the first time in his life that he ever had. But darkened windows were all that met his hungry gaze. After a moment, he pulled the Jeep back onto the road and drove home.

Inside the house, Allison had made it to her room without being seen by Winnie. She took a shower, with water as hot as she could stand it, to wash away the scent and feel of Gene Nelson. She washed her hair as well. Her body felt bruised and torn, but she couldn't bring herself to tell Winnie what had happened. She was going to have to invent an argument or something to explain her sudden departure. But whatever happened, she couldn't stay here any longer. Even the horror of the past few weeks and the fear of being hounded by the media were preferable to ever having to see Gene again. He hated her. She'd made him hate her by lying to him. He must feel terrible now, too, knowing the truth about her. He'd said he didn't play around with virgins, and she'd made a liar out of him.

She lay down, but she didn't sleep. Her mind went over and over that painful episode in the line cabin until she was utterly sick. The worst of it was that Gene was right. It was her fault. She'd ignored Winnie's warnings about Gene and the danger of physical attraction. Now she understood, too late, what it was all about. She'd never dreamed that she could be so hungry for a man that principles and morals could be totally forgotten. Now she knew. She wondered if she'd ever be able to forget what she'd done. Loving him didn't seem to excuse her behavior, or justify her submission anymore.

She got up before daylight and packed. The phone rang long before she dressed and went downstairs, but apparently it wasn't for her, because she wasn't disturbed.

She put her hair up in a bun and dressed in her sedate gray dress with matching high heels for the trip to Arizona. With a glance at her too-pale face in the mirror, she went in to breakfast and pasted a smile on her lips.

But there was no one there. She searched the house and found a scribbled note from Winnie. "Gone to hospital," she read. "Dwight hurt in wreck."

She caught her breath. Poor Winnie! And poor Dwight! She picked up the phone and called the hospital immediately, having found the number in the telephone directory. Fortunately there wasn't more than one hospital in Pryor.

She got the floor nurse on Dwight's ward and talked to her. After introducing herself, she explained about Dwight and Winnie and the nurse was sympathetic enough to tell her what had happened. When she hung up, she knew it was going to be impossible for her to leave. Dwight was in intensive care and he might die. She was trapped. She couldn't leave Winnie at a time like this, even if it meant having to endure Gene's hatred in the process.

Eight

Winnie came home at lunch, red-eyed and wilted, supported by her worried mother.

"Oh, Winnie, I'm so sorry," Allison said, hugging her friend warmly. "Is there any change?"

"Not yet." Winnie wept. "Allie, I can't bear to lose him! I can't!"

"Head injuries are tricky," Allison said quietly. "He's in a coma, but that doesn't mean he won't come out of it. I've seen some near-fatal injuries that recovered fully. Give it time."

"I'll go mad!" the blonde wailed.

Allison hugged her again. "No, you won't. Come on, I've made lunch. I'll bet you're both starved."

"I certainly am," Mrs. Manley said gently. She smiled at Allison. "Bless you for thinking of food. We really hadn't."

"I can understand why. What happened?"

"Nobody knows. The car he was driving went down a ravine. They only found him early this morning. Gene and Marie are at the hospital. Gene looks really bad," Winnie said.

Allison averted her face before anyone could see that she did, too, and make any embarrassing connections. "I'll pour the coffee," she said.

She didn't want to go to the hospital with them, but Winnie pleaded, so she did.

When they walked into the waiting room, only Marie was there, and Allison thanked her lucky stars. She hugged Marie and murmured all the comforting things she could think of. Then she went in search of the floor nurse she'd talked to on the phone, while Winnie and Mrs. Manley sat with Marie.

Tina Gates was in charge of the intensive care unit, a twenty-two-year veteran of nursing arts. She welcomed Allison and showed her through the ward, pausing at Dwight's bed.

"He's bad," she told Allison. "But he's a fighter, like the rest of his family, and strong-willed. I think he'll come out of it."

"I hope so," Allison said gently, staring at Dwight's unnaturally pale face. "My best friend loves him very much."

"Sometimes love is what it takes." She continued the tour, and they came back to Dwight's cubical when they finished. "If you ever want a job, we've got a place for you," she told Allison. "Help is hard to get out here, and you're more qualified than even

I am. I never had the opportunity to go on and get my degree in nursing arts.''

"I was lucky," Allison said. "My parents sacrificed a lot for my education. It's important work, and I love it. I don't know that I could get used to the routine in a hospital. I'm too accustomed to primitive conditions. But I appreciate the offer, all the same.''

"I'll repeat it at intervals, if you promise to consider it," Tina promised, smiling. "This is pretty country, and there are some nice folks here. You might like it.''

"I already do. But I made a promise to my parents that I'd carry on the work they did," Allison said finally. "I don't like to break promises.''

"Actually, neither do...look!''

Tina went quickly to Dwight's side and watched him move restlessly. His eyes opened and he groaned.

"Head...hurts," he mumbled.

"Hallelujah!" Tina grinned. "If your head hurts, Mr. Nelson, it means you're alive. I'll get Dr. Jackson right now!''

"I'll go and tell Winnie. Dwight, I'm glad you're back with us," she said gently, touching his arm where the IV was attached. "They'll give you something for the pain. Just try to relax and don't move around too much.''

He looked up at her, licking dry lips. "Gene?" he whispered.

Her face closed up. "Do you want to see him?''

"Yes.''

"I'll try to find him. Rest, now." She patted his hand and walked out, all nerves.

Gene was in the waiting room when she came out. He stiffened as she approached, but Allison pretended not to notice. After the night before, it was all she could do to stay in the same room with him without breaking down and crying.

"He's out of the coma," she said, talking to Winnie and Marie. "They're getting the doctor. I think he'll be all right."

"Oh, thank God!" Winnie burst out, and Marie laughed and cried as the two women hugged each other.

"Your first-aid training qualifies you to make prognoses, does it?" Gene drawled suddenly with cold mockery. Having her deliberately ignore him had hurt him terribly.

"First-aid training?" Winnie asked, frowning. "Gene, she's a registered nurse, didn't she tell you?"

Gene scowled. "A nurse!"

"A graduate nurse, with a college degree," Winnie said. "You didn't tell him?" she asked Allison.

Allison's eyes warned her not to give anything else away. "There was no need to," she said simply. She didn't want him to know about the life she'd led. "Dwight is asking for you," she said.

"He wants to talk business," Winnie muttered. "Well, that can wait. I want to see him first. Marie, come on, we'll go together."

"But the doctor…" Allison began.

"We'll ask first," Winnie promised, dragging a smiling Marie along with her.

Allison was left alone with Gene, who was lighting a cigarette with curt, economical movements.

"A nurse. No wonder you were so good at patching people up," he said absently, lifting the cigarette to his mouth to take a heavy draw from it. Even Dwight's miraculous return to consciousness didn't quite register through the shock. He glared at her. "How many other secrets are you keeping?" he asked bitterly. She hadn't trusted him at all. Did everyone know things about her that he didn't?

"Enough, I suppose," she said, folding her hands in front of her. She turned away from him and stared out the window.

"I thought you were leaving today."

"So did I. Don't worry. This is just a temporary setback. The minute Dwight's off the critical list, I'll be on the next plane out."

His eyes narrowed. Was that what she thought? That he couldn't wait to get rid of her? Seeing her did play havoc with his conscience, but probably it was worse for her. Why hadn't she told him she was a qualified nurse? And what were those other secrets she was keeping? She hadn't shared anything with him, except her body, and she hadn't enjoyed that. It would haunt him forever that he'd taken his pleasure at her expense. Poor little thing, all she'd given him since they met was tenderness and concern and compassion. And for that, he'd given her a nightmare experience that would scar her.

Guilt was riding him hard. It was the first time in memory that he'd ever hurt a woman in bed, and he didn't like the feeling. His teeth ground together. If only she'd told him! He'd have made her glory in that sweet sacrifice. Of course, he had to admit that it could have been worse. He'd aroused her totally, and he'd treated her like a virgin, as if maybe subconsciously he had known. A man without scruples could have done her a lot more damage. He frowned, thinking about Allison in bed with some other man. It made him livid with jealousy.

"A nurse, of all things," he said curtly, glaring at her. "It's a miracle that you reached your present age intact. Don't they teach you anything about sex in nurses' training?"

She went scarlet and wouldn't look at him. "It isn't the same as reading about it," she said stiffly.

His jaw clenched. "No doubt. You little fool, if I'd known, I could have made you faint with the pleasure! God knows, I had the experience to give you that. I hurt you. My conscience is giving me hell. Damn it, Allison, if I'd known, I could have stopped!"

She turned, her eyes shy but knowing. "Could you, Gene?" she asked sadly.

He averted his eyes to the wall. No, of course he couldn't have. But it made him feel better to think so. He took another draw from the cigarette. "Dwight will have to have around-the-clock nursing when he comes home. He's got some internal injuries and a busted rib besides the concussion."

"It shouldn't be too difficult finding someone," she said slowly, although she had her doubts after what Tina Gates had said about the shortage of nurses around here.

He whirled and stared at her. "He likes you." Was he out of his mind, he wondered? The very last thing she'd agree to was a job that put her near him. But the thought was intriguing. Having her in his home, near him, being able to look at her whenever he liked would be so sweet. He caught his breath at the very thought of it.

Allison was catching her own breath. She didn't want to be near him, not at any price. "No," she said hastily. "No, I can't do it. I have to go back to Arizona."

He moved toward her, and she backed up a step, afraid to be close to him again. What had happened once was never going to be allowed to happen again.

Gene stopped. He understood that timid retreat. He'd hurt her, mentally and physically. She had every right to be intimidated by him.

"Dwight needs you," he said softly. Charm had never meant much to him before, but if he could lure her home with him, he might have a chance that she'd begin to trust him. "Winnie would be grateful," he coaxed. "And so would Marie and I."

"You needn't pretend that you want me around, Gene," she replied miserably. "You can find someone else to sit with Dwight."

"He has nothing to do with you and me," he said after a minute, his eyes narrow and steady on her face. "He's my brother, honey. I love him."

That got to her when nothing else had. She clasped her hands tightly together. "I thought you'd decided you weren't part of his family anymore," she murmured.

He sighed. "So I had. Until I heard he'd been hurt. Strange how nothing else seems to matter when so-

meone's near death. I thought of all the good times
we had as kids, all the games we played together, all
the mischief we got into.'' He raised the cigarette to
his thin lips with a faint smile. ''Even if there wasn't
much blood tying us together, we were the best of
friends. Marie and I fight, but we'd die for each other.
I guess I've been living inside myself without a
thought to how it affected them.'' He looked straight
at her. ''It's still hard for me. But I think we can work
it out now, if I don't have to worry about somebody
to take care of Dwight. The hospital is short staffed.''

''Tina told me,'' she said. She wrapped her arms
around her breasts and turned away, head bent.

He moved closer, keeping some distance between
them so that she wouldn't feel uncomfortable. ''You
can't regret what happened any more than I do, sweetheart,'' he said unexpectedly, and in a tone that made
her legs tremble. ''I'm sorry.''

Her eyes closed. ''It was my fault, too,'' she replied huskily, shaken by his compassion and the soft
endearment. ''Can we...not talk about it anymore,
please?''

''Can I assume that since you've had medical training, you knew how to take care of yourself after what
we did?'' he persisted, holding his breath while he
waited for her reply. He knew he hadn't taken any
precautions, and he was pretty sure she hadn't. But
he wanted to know.

She didn't look at him. ''It wasn't a dangerous time
of the month, if that's what you're asking,'' she said,
coloring.

He let out a heavy sigh. "Allison," he said softly, "that wasn't what I asked."

She bit her lower lip. "Afterward is too late to do anything," she said, averting her gaze to the window.

"I see." He moved again, towering over her. "Six weeks...is that how long it takes to be certain?" he asked quietly.

She didn't look up, but she nodded.

He started to speak, but anything he said would be the wrong thing now. His shoulders lifted and fell in a strangely impotent gesture and he moved back to the chairs.

The thought of a child scared him to death. He couldn't imagine what they'd do if they'd created a life together during that frenzied coupling. He didn't want a child to suffer for his lapse. He was terrified because of his father's character, sick at the thought of passing those genes onto a child. It wasn't rational, but it was how he felt. God, there couldn't be a child!

But even as he dreaded that thought, his eyes sought Allison and he scowled thoughtfully. She had a built-in maternal instinct. He could imagine her with a baby in her arms, suckling at her breast...

The sudden, fierce arousal of his body made him gasp audibly. God, what a thing to trigger it! But the more he thought about Allison's slim body growing big with a child, the worse it got. He got up from the chair and left the room without another word, leaving Allison to stare after him with sad curiosity. He couldn't imagine what was wrong with him!

Dwight was glad to see him, and Gene was relieved that his baby brother wasn't going to meet his maker just yet. He looked at the face so like his, and yet so unalike, and smiled indulgently as he held the other man's hand tightly for a minute.

"Need anything you haven't got?" he asked.

Dwight smiled through a drugged haze. "Not really, thanks. You handle things for us while I'm here, okay? I think I've made a real mess of the books."

"You don't know what I've done to the daily routine with the livestock," Gene confessed with a grin.

"Dad sure fouled us up, didn't he?" Dwight groaned. "I know he never meant it to wind up this way. He knew I couldn't handle finances. Why saddle me with it?"

"We'll never know," Gene replied. "We just have to make the best of it."

"No, we don't. We can go back to the way we were doing things before Dad died. If we both agree to it, we can have a contract drawn up and the will won't be binding. I've already asked our attorneys."

"You didn't mention that to me," Gene reminded him.

Dwight shifted. "You weren't ready to listen. I know it hit you hard, finding out about the past. But I figured when you were ready, we could talk about it." He winced. "Head hurts real bad, Gene."

"I know." He patted the younger man's shoulder. "I'm trying to talk Allison into nursing you at home. Would you like that?"

He smiled weakly. "Yes. They'd let me go home earlier if I had my own nurse."

"Did you know she was one?" Gene asked, scowling.

"Sure. Winnie told me. And about her parents. Incredible, that she got out at all, isn't it...? Gene, I need a shot real bad."

"I'll go and ask for you," Gene replied, puzzled about what Dwight had started to say. What about Allison's parents? Had there been anything unusual about the way they died? And what was that about it being incredible that Allison got out? Out of where? What? He glowered with frustration. Well, he was going to find out one way or the other. He was tired of being kept in the dark.

Winnie asked, and so did Marie, if Allison would nurse Dwight. It had been hard enough to refuse Gene, but there was no way she could refuse Winnie. What she didn't know was how she was going to survive a week or more under Gene's roof when Dwight went home.

"You've been different lately," Winnie said several days later, when Allison had put some things into a small bag to take to the Nelson home.

"Different, how?" she hedged.

"Quieter. Less interested in the world. Have you and Gene had a fight? Is that it?"

"Yes," Allison said, because it was easier to admit that than to tell the truth. "A very bad falling out. I was going to leave the morning that Dwight got hurt."

"Oh, Allie." Winnie sat down on the bed where Allison was folding clothes. "I'm sorry. But if Gene wants you to stay with Dwight—and Marie said it was his idea—he can't be holding a grudge."

"He has a lot of reason to hold one," Allison confessed. She lowered her eyes to the floor. "It's better that I don't see too much of him, that's all."

Marie's eyes narrowed. "Would this have anything to do with Dale Branigan?"

Allison lifted her head. "How did you know about her?"

"Everybody knows about her." Winnie grimaced. "She's been after Gene for a long time—just like most of the single women around here. But she was more blatant with it, and she's a very modern girl. Gene wasn't the first or the last, but she's persistent."

"Yes, I noticed."

"I gave you a bad impression of Gene at the start," Winnie began. "I just wanted to protect you, but I wasn't quite fair to him. Gene can't help being attractive, and I hear he's just plain dynamite in bed. Women chase him. They always have. But since he met you, he's not as wild as he was—he's calmed down a good bit. It's just that he can't shake his old reputation, and I didn't want yours damaged by it."

"Thanks," Allison said quietly. "I know you meant well." She managed not to blush at Winnie's remark about how Gene was in bed. She knew all too well that he was dynamite, and if she hadn't been a virgin, maybe it would have gone on feeling as sweet as it had when he was just kissing and stroking her body.

But maybe that really was all sex was supposed to feel like, for a woman. Maybe it was the preliminary part that made women give in. She sighed. If that was what sex felt like, she wasn't in any rush to experience it again, despite the brief pleasure that had led to it.

Winnie drove her over to the Nelson house, where Dwight was tucked up in bed with every conceivable amusement scattered around him. He had his own color TV, VCR, all the latest movies, a CD player, dozens of up-to-date compact discs and a veritable library of the latest bestsellers.

"Talk about the man who has everything," Allison said, smiling at him.

"Not quite everything," Dwight said with weak humor. "My head could use a replacement."

"You'll get better day by day. Don't be too impatient. I'll take very good care of you."

"Thanks." He hesitated, staring up at her with his vivid blue eyes. "I get the feeling that you and Gene are having some problems. In view of that, I really appreciate the sacrifice you're making for me," he added.

She smiled wanly. "Gene and I had a difference of opinion, that's all," she said, trying to downplay it.

"In other words, he tried to get you into bed and you said no." He chuckled when she went scarlet. "Good for you. It will do him good to have the wind knocked out of him."

She didn't say anything. Let him think what he liked. She couldn't bear having anyone find out what had really caused her difference of opinion with Gene. It was a godsend that he was out with the cattle, and she didn't have to see him until she'd settled in.

Winnie was there for supper, visiting with Marie

while Allison got Dwight up and ready for the meal that would be served on a tray in his room.

"Gene won't be in until late," Marie said as she helped Winnie and Allison fix a tray. "I'm sorry this had to happen to Dwight, but it's a good thing, in a way. It's brought Gene to the realization that he's still part of this family. I wouldn't take a million dollars for that. He's actually being civil to me, and he's been wonderful to Dwight."

"Sometimes it takes a near tragedy to make us appreciate what we have," she agreed. "You two have a nice supper. I'll come down and get something later. I'm not really hungry right now."

"Okay," Marie said, and smiled. "There's plenty of stuff in the fridge, and if there's anything you need in your room, let us know."

"I'll do that. Thank you, Marie."

"No. Thank *you*," the other woman replied, impulsively hugging her. "You don't know what a load you've taken off our minds."

"Yes, she does," Winnie said warmly, smiling at Allison. "She's very special."

"I'm leaving." Allison laughed. "See you later."

She arranged Dwight's tray and sat down by the bed while he maneuvered his utensils through a pained fog.

"Isn't Gene home yet?" he asked.

She shook her head. "Marie said he'd be late," she replied, hating to talk about him at all.

Dwight caught that note in her voice. He studied her curiously. "You haven't told Gene anything about yourself. Why?"

She couldn't answer that. In the beginning it had been because she didn't want to scare him off. Now, she didn't see any logic in it. She'd be gone soon and Gene wanted no more of her.

"I don't know," she told Dwight. "I suppose the way I've lived has taught me to keep things to myself. My parents were the kind of people who didn't like whiners. They believed in honor and hard work and love." She smiled sadly. "I'll miss them all my life."

"I miss my father that way," he replied. "So do the others. Gene, too. Dad was the only father he really knew."

"What about Gene's real father?" she asked softly.

He started to speak and hesitated. "You'd better ask Gene that," he said. "He and I are getting along better than we have in a long time. I don't want to interfere in his business."

"I can understand that. Can I get you anything?" she asked.

He shook his head. "Thanks. I think I could sleep a little now."

She straightened his pillow with a smile. "I'll get something to read and be nearby if you need me. You've got medicine for the pain. Please don't be nervous about asking for it if you need it. Your body can't heal itself and fight off the pain all at once in your weakened condition. All right?"

"You make it sound simple."

"Most things are. It's people that complicate it all. Sleep well."

Winnie came up later to check on him, and volunteered to sit with Dwight while Allison went down to get herself a sandwich.

Marie had gone to a movie with one of her friends since Allison and Winnie were staying with Dwight. She had, she told them, needed the diversion. It had been a traumatic few days.

Allison understood that. She'd had a pretty traumatic few days herself.

She went downstairs and fixed herself a sandwich in the kitchen, grateful that Marie had left her half a pot of fresh coffee. She ate at the kitchen table, liking the cozy atmosphere, with all Marie's green plants giving the yellow and white decor of the room the feel of a conservatory. She was just starting on her second cup of hot black coffee when the back door opened and Gene came in.

He looked tired, his face under his wide-brimmed hat hard with new lines. He was wearing dusty boots and jeans and bat-wing chaps, as he had been that day Allison had met him in town, but despite the dust, he was still the most physically devastating man Allison had ever met.

He paused at the table, absently unfastening his chaps while he studied her. She was wearing the gray dress he'd seen her in several times, with her hair up and no makeup, and she looked as tired as he felt.

"Worn-out, little one?" he asked gently.

His unexpected compassion all but made her cry. She took a sip of hot coffee to steady herself. "I'm okay." She glanced at him and away, shyly. He was incredibly handsome, with that lean dark face and black hair and glittering peridot eyes. "You look pretty worn-out yourself."

He tossed his Stetson onto the sideboard and smoothed back his black hair. "I've been helping brand cattle." He straddled a chair and folded his arms over the back. "Got another cup?"

"Of course." She poured him a cup of hot coffee. "Want anything in it?" she asked.

He shook his head. "Thanks." He took it from her, noticing how she avoided letting her hand come into contact with his. But he caught her free hand lightly, clasping it in his as he searched her face. "Can't you look at me, sweetheart?" he asked when she kept her eyes downcast.

The endearment went through her like lightning. She didn't dare let him see her eyes. "Let me go, please," she said, and tugged gently at her hand.

He released her with reluctance, watching her as she went back to her own chair and sat down. He no longer had any doubts about her reaction to him. He wrapped his lean hands around his coffee cup and flexed his shoulders, strained from hours in the saddle and back-breaking work as they threw calves to brand them.

"How's Dwight?" he asked after a minute.

"He's doing very well," she replied. "He's still in a lot of pain, of course. Winnie's sitting with him right now. Marie's gone to a movie."

"I haven't said it, but I appreciate having you stay with him. Especially under the circumstances."

She sipped her coffee quietly, darting a quick glance up at him. He was watching her with steady, narrow, unblinking eyes. She averted her gaze to her coffee cup again.

"I'm doing it for Winnie," she said finally.

"That goes without saying." He put his cup down and lit a cigarette, reaching behind him on the sideboard for an ashtray. "How long will it take, do you think, before he's on his feet again?"

"I don't know," she said. "You'd have to ask the doctor about that."

He blew out a cloud of smoke and watched it drift across the room. He'd driven himself hard today, trying not to think about Allison and what he'd done. But it hadn't worked. Here she was, and sitting with her was the first peace he'd known all day. She had a calming effect on him. She made him feel at ease with himself and the world around him. It was a feeling he'd never known before. His emotions had gone wild with Hank Nelson's death and the subsequent revelations about his past.

He thought about his real father and the shame it would bring on him to have people know what kind of parent he'd had. But the sting of that knowledge seemed to have lessened. Now he could look at Allison and none of the anguish he'd known seemed to matter anymore. All he could think about was how it had been with her during the time they'd spent together, her softness in his arms, her gentle voice full of compassion and warmth. But he'd killed all that. He'd reduced what they were building together into a feverish sexual fling, without meaning or purpose. That was how she was bound to see it, and it wasn't

true. He'd used women before, of course he had, but
Allison wasn't an interlude. She was…everything.

He looked at her with soft wonder. She couldn't
know how she'd changed him. She probably wouldn't
care, even if she knew it. The more he saw of her,
the more he realized how genuinely kind she was.
He'd never met a woman like her. He knew he never
would again.

"I've been a fool about my family, Allison," he
said suddenly, his dark brows knitted together as he
stared at her. "I think I went mad when I found out
how I'd been lied to all these years. Hurt pride, arrogance, I don't know. Whatever it was, I've just
come to my senses."

"I'm glad about that," she replied. "You have a
nice family. They shouldn't have to pay for things
they never did."

"I've come to that conclusion myself." He finished
the cigarette and his coffee and put out the stub in
the ashtray. "Are you going to be able to forgive what
I've done to you?" he asked suddenly.

Her heart jumped at the question. But in all fairness, she couldn't let him take all the blame. Nobody
held a gun on her and made her do it, she knew. That
one lapse could have cost her her career as a missionary if anyone had found out about it, but she
couldn't have blamed him totally even then. She was
pretty lucky that they hadn't been seen at that line
cabin, she supposed. "You didn't do anything that I
didn't invite," she said dully. "It doesn't matter."

Her reply caught him on the raw. "You might have

my child inside your body, and it doesn't matter?''
he asked icily.

She flushed. "It isn't likely," she said stubbornly.

His chest rose and fell roughly. Even now she
wouldn't put all the blame on him. His lean hand
speared across the table and gently slid into hers,
holding it warmly. "I'm sorry I made it into something you'd rather not remember," he said solemnly.
"It shouldn't have been like that, your first time. The
least a man owes a virgin is satisfaction. All I gave
you was pain."

She colored furiously and drew back her hand. "I
have to get back to Dwight," she said huskily. "Good
night, Gene."

She stood, but so did he, moving around the table
so fast that she didn't see him coming until he had
her gently by the shoulders, his tall, fit body looming
over her.

"Do you hate me?" he asked abruptly. "No subterfuge, no half-truths. I need to know."

She swallowed. "No. I...don't hate you."

He let out a heavy sigh. "Thank God." He bent
and brushed his mouth over her eyelids, closing them
with aching tenderness. His hands held her, but not
in any confining way, and he didn't move a fraction
of an inch closer or threaten her mouth with his lips.

"Good night, little one," he said softly, lifting his
head. There was something new in his eyes, in his
voice, in the way he touched her. He knew it and was
stunned by it. Women came and went in his life, but
this one spun a cocoon of love around him and made
him whole. He wanted her as he'd never wanted any-

thing else. But it wasn't going to be easy. His eyes
fell to her stomach and darkened. A child. He found
the thought of a child not nearly as frightening as he
had. He could almost picture a little boy with dark
hair and green eyes, following him around. A mini-
ature of himself in small blue jeans and little sneakers.
His heart lurched. Allison would be wonderful with
a child. And maybe genes weren't so important.
Maybe it wouldn't matter about his father. But the
manner of the child's possible conception bothered
him and he frowned.

His hands contracted. "A baby shouldn't be made
like that," he said huskily. "Not as a consequence.
It should be planned. Wanted. God in heaven, why
didn't I stop?"

He let go of her all at once, and turned, leaving the
kitchen like a wild man. He sounded bitter and furiously angry. Probably he hated her. She couldn't
blame him for that. He might even think she'd deliberately done without precautions to trap him into a
marriage he didn't want. Tears stung her eyes. All the
same, he'd been worried that she might hate him, and
that gave her a little solace. She finished her coffee,
unplugged the pot and cleaned it, washed the few
dishes and went back up to sit with Dwight.

Nine

The next day, Allison went outside for the first time since she'd been in residence, to clear her head while Marie spent a few minutes with her brother.

It was a beautiful day, warm and sultry, and there was so much to see. Puppies and kittens, ducks and chickens were everywhere, not to mention the bulls and cows and steers and horses. Corrals were spaced beyond the house and its small kitchen garden, down a dirt road. She strolled along in her jeans and yellow T-shirt with her long hair drifting on the breeze. Even with all that had happened, she loved it here. But she knew her stay was limited—she had to think about leaving.

She'd been given some time off to cope with her parents' death, and avoid the press, but soon she'd have to go back to work. It was a good thing that she'd face that problem in Arizona and not here, because there was a morals clause in her contract. But nobody knew, she reminded herself. Nobody knew except Gene and herself.

She was worrying about Gene's sudden avoidance of her today when a voice hailed her from the corral.

She turned, frowning, to find a lean, wickedly smiling redheaded cowhand leaning against the fence. His eyes gave her a lazy appraisal and there was something vaguely insulting about the blatant way he sized her up.

"Miss Hathoway, isn't it?" he drawled. "Thought I recognized you."

She started. *Recognized her?* "Were you at the barbecue?" she asked, trying to be polite.

The man laughed, weaving a little as he pushed himself away from the fence. He approached her and she could smell the whiskey on his breath. "No, I don't get invited to that sort of socializing. I meant, I recognized you from the other night. In the line cabin. You were there with the boss."

Her face went stark white. She was quite literally at a loss for words.

He laughed unsteadily, moving closer, but she backed away before he could reach for her. That had obviously been his intention, because he looked surprised that she avoided his outstretched hands.

"No stomach for a common ranch hand, is that it?" he jeered. "You were hot enough for the boss. Of course, he's got money."

"Please!" she cried huskily, scarlet in the face that she and Gene should have been seen—like that!

"The boss won't have much to do with you these days, though, will he, Miss High and Mighty?" he taunted. "I heard what he said. Mad as hell that you were a virgin, wasn't he? Not his usual kind of woman, for sure, he likes 'em worldly. Now me," he said, stalking her again, smiling, "I like innocents. I'd take my sweet time with you, pretty thing, and you wouldn't be looking like the end of the world afterward. He must have been in one hell of a rush. You weren't in there ten minutes."

Allison put her hand to her mouth and turned, running wildly for the house with tears in her eyes. She didn't know what to do. It terrified her that the cowboy might tell someone else what he knew. At least he hadn't seen them, or she knew he'd have taunted her with that, too. But he knew! He'd overheard what Gene said! And now he'd spread that horrible gossip around. She could imagine having her name bandied around the bunkhouse all night. And that wasn't the worst of it. What if it got around the community? Her reputation would be lost forever and her job along with it. The least breath of scandal attached to her name would cost her everything. She hadn't considered the potential for disaster, but now all her mistakes were coming home to roost.

She went back into the house and stayed there, taking a few minutes in her room to wash her face and get her nerves back together before she went to Dwight's room to check on him. It was almost time for his medicine.

If she'd hoped nobody would notice her turmoil, she was doomed to failure.

"What's wrong?" Winnie asked, concerned. "Allie, you're so pale!"

The temptation to tell her friend was great, but it wouldn't be fair to share the burden now. Winnie had enough to worry about with Dwight. She forced a smile. "I feel a little queasy," she said. "I think it was the sausage I had for breakfast. I love it, but sometimes it upsets my stomach."

"Tomorrow, you'll have steak," Dwight said with a weak smile. "I promise. Tell Gene to shoot you a cow."

She started just at the mention of Gene's name. How could she face him, ever, after what that terrible man had said? How would he react if he knew one of his men was making crude remarks to her? She sighed. After the way he'd walked away from her so angrily that night in the kitchen, he probably wouldn't say anything. He might think she deserved it. After all, he'd been very vocal about Dale Branigan and his contempt for her after he'd slept with her.

She gave Dwight his medicine and put on a fairly convincing act from then on. But when she was alone in her room, she cried until she thought her heart would break. She was paying a very high price for the one indiscretion of her life, and learning a hard lesson about how easy it was to tarnish a heretofore spotless reputation. She thought about how hard her parents had worked to invest her with a sense of morality, and she'd let them down so badly. Maybe it was as well that they'd never have to know about her downfall. But she could have talked to her mother about it, and there would have been no censure, no condemnation. Her mother was a loving, gentle woman who always looked for the best in everyone. She cried all the harder, missing her.

For the next few days, she didn't go outside at all. But inevitably, Winnie noticed it and asked why. Allison made up a story about not wanting to be out of earshot of Dwight. But Winnie told Marie. And Marie told Gene.

He alone knew that Allison might simply be avoiding him. But he'd been away from the ranch for a couple of days on business, and that wouldn't explain why she was staying inside while he was gone. He almost said something to her about it. Her abrupt departure from any room he entered stopped him. She obviously wanted no part of his company, so he forced himself not to invade her privacy. All the while, he was cursing himself for what he'd done to her. Even he, a relative stranger, could see the change in her since that night in the line cabin. She was almost a different person, so quiet and shy that she might have been a mouse. She never entered into conversations with the rest of the family, or laughed, or did anything except be professional as she charted Dwight's progress and talked to the doctor who checked on him several times a week. She didn't look at Gene or speak to him, and when he tried to make conversation with her, she found a reason to go somewhere else. His pride and ego took a hard blow from her attitude, even if he understood it. Women had never avoided him. Quite the contrary. Of course, he'd never hurt anyone the way he'd hurt Allison.

Winnie and Marie finally browbeat her into going

into Pryor with them to shop. She felt fairly safe about
going there, sure that she wouldn't run into anyone
who knew her.

She was wrong. Dale Branigan was shopping, too,
in the boutique where Marie and Winnie took Allison.
She caught sight of the older woman and with a
purely cattish smile, Dale maneuvered closer.

"Nice to see you again, Miss Hathoway," she said.
"Ben's doing nicely, thanks to your quick thinking
at the bar that night."

"I'm glad to hear it," Allison said pleasantly.

Dale gave the other woman's gray dress a demean-
ing scrutiny, shrugging when she realized how much
prettier she was in a pink dotted Swiss affair that flat-
tered her figure.

"I hear Gene's gone off you after that one night,"
she said out of the blue.

"I beg your pardon?" Allison asked reluctantly.

"After he slept with you in the line cabin," she
said carelessly, smiling at Allison's gasped shock.
"Didn't you know? It's all over town. You can't expect a man like Danny Rance to keep his mouth shut.
He's a bigger gossip than most women. He really laid
it on thick about you and Gene. Too bad. You should
have held out for a wedding ring." She sighed the-
atrically. "By the way, there's a wire-service reporter
in town. He's looking for some woman missionary
who escaped from Central America in a hail of bullets. Someone said she'd left a trail that led here."

"Really?" Allison's hands were shaking. "Well, it
could hardly be me, could it?" she asked huskily.

Dale laughed. "Not if you're giving out with Gene,

it couldn't," she said mockingly. "Hardly a mission-ary's nature, is it?"

"Hardly. Excuse me." Allison went out the door and got into the car without a word to Marie or Win-nie. She sat in shock, her body shaking, her face paper white as she tried to cope with what that malicious woman had said to her. She was branded. Really branded. She'd never get her job back. She'd have no place to go. Her family was dead, and now she was almost certainly going to lose the only work she'd ever wanted to do. It was inevitable that the wire-service reporter would track her to the Nelson place, inevitable that Dale or someone like her would relate the whole sordid story of her one-night stand with Gene. She'd given in to temptation and lost every-thing. If she'd had a lesser will, she'd probably have gone right off a cliff. She didn't know what she was going to do. Oh, please, God, she prayed silently. Please forgive me. Please help me!

Winnie and Marie belatedly noticed her absence and came looking for her.

"Are you all right?" Winnie frowned. "I saw Dale Branigan talking to you. What did she say?"

"Something about Gene, no doubt," Marie said heavily as they started the drive home. "She's so jeal-ous it's sick. I'm sorry, Allison, I should have hustled you out of there the minute I saw her."

"It's all right. She was just…telling me something I already knew."

"There's a reporter in town," Winnie said uneas-ily. "That was what she said, wasn't it?"

"Yes. I may have a few days before he finds me,"

she said with defeat in her whole look. "It doesn't matter anymore. I don't have anything left to lose."

"What are you talking about?" Winnie demanded. "You've got your job, your future…!"

"I don't have anything." Allison pushed back wisps of hair with shaking hands. "I've ruined my life."

"How?"

Allison just shook her head and stared out the window. She was too hurt and upset to even talk.

When they got back to the ranch she went to her room and locked the door. She couldn't face anyone just yet.

"What's wrong with her?" Marie asked quietly when she and Winnie were drinking coffee while Dwight slept. "Something's upset her terribly. I wonder what Dale said to her? Could it just be the reporter who's got her upset?"

"I don't know." Winnie sipped coffee, aware of the front door opening and closing. "Surely, Gene won't let him come here, will he?"

"I won't let who come here?" Gene asked abruptly, taking off his work gloves as he paused in the doorway.

"That reporter," Marie said. "The one who's looking for Allison."

He scowled. "What reporter? And why is he looking for our houseguest?"

Winnie hesitated. She exchanged glances with Marie and grimaced. "I guess you'd better hear it all. Allison isn't going to tell you, but someone needs to. You'd better sit down."

He sprawled in the armchair next to the sofa and lit a cigarette. "All right," he said, his green eyes solemn. It would be almost a relief to know it all. He'd had a feeling from the very first that Allison wasn't what she seemed, although he had one strong premonition that he wasn't going to like what he found out.

"Allison and her parents were sent to Central America to set up a small clinic in one of the rural provinces," Winnie began. "It was a war zone, and inevitably, two opposing factions threatened the village."

"What were they doing in Central America?" Gene interrupted.

Winnie blinked. "Why, they were missionaries."

Gene's face went several shades paler and his jaw clenched. "All of them?" he asked in a choked tone. "Allison, too?"

"Yes," Winnie replied, confirming his worst fears.

He ran a hand through his hair, his eyes blank. Now it all made sense. No wonder she'd been so naïve, so trusting. He closed his eyes. If the guilt had been there before, it was almost unbearable now. A missionary. He'd seduced a missionary! "Finish it," he said stiffly, opening his eyes to glare at her.

"They were taken prisoner," Winnie said slowly. "Allison's parents were shot to death right beside her, and the firing squad had taken aim at her when the opposing force marched in and spared her. She was smuggled out of the country before the invasion of that international peacekeeping force. She has information that nobody else has, and that's why the media's been after her. She came here to heal, Gene.''

He'd gone rigid during that revelation. When Winnie finished, he got up out of his chair without a word and went out the front door. He didn't want anyone to see what he felt at the thought of bullets tearing into that gentle, loving woman. He felt something wet in his eyes and kept walking while stark terror ran over his body like fire. Incredible, Dwight had said. No. Not incredible. A miracle. Allison believed in miracles, she'd told him once, and now he knew why. She was alive because of one.

The sound of approaching voices disturbed his thoughts. He wasn't really listening, it was just some of the hands heading into the bunkhouse for lunch. But then one loud, slurred voice caught his attention.

Rance, he thought angrily, drinking again. He'd warned the man once. Now he was going to have to do something about it. The hands knew he wouldn't tolerate alcohol during working hours.

Just as he crushed out his cigarette and started around the barn toward the bunkhouse, he heard what Rance was saying.

''She wouldn't give me the time of day,'' the man snarled. ''Can you imagine that? She didn't mind rolling around in that line cabin with the boss, but she was too good to let me touch her. Dale hates her guts, and I can see why. Well, it's all over town about the high and mighty Miss Hathoway and Nelson, and before I'm through...''

His voice trailed off as the object of his venom

walked into the bunkhouse with an expression on his face that made the rest of the men scatter.

"Now, boss," Rance began hesitantly, because he knew the set of the older man's lean body and the glitter of those green eyes from long experience.

"You son of a…!" The last word was muffled by a huge fist as Gene knocked the cowboy to the floor and dived after him. They demolished chairs in the struggle, but it was no contest. Gene was quicker and more muscular than the young cowboy, and he had the advantage of murderous anger.

He pulled Rance up from the floor and knocked him through the open bunkhouse door and out into the dirt, and was going after him again when one of the older hands stepped in front of him.

"He's had enough, boss," the man said gently, keeping his voice low and calm. "You got the point across. No need to tear his arms off. None of us listened to his venom. A blind man would know that Miss Hathoway's a lady."

Gene was breathing heavily. He looked from the half conscious man on the ground to the one who was speaking, his green eyes hot and wild. He took a deep breath to steady himself. "If anyone else asks, Miss Hathoway is my *fiancée*," he emphasized the word, looking at each cowboy's face individually with an expression that was calm and dangerous all at once. "I may deserve that kind of malicious gossip, but she doesn't. She's a missionary. A man who *is* a man doesn't belittle a woman of her sort!"

The men looked shamefaced. They stood uncomfortably congregated with downcast eyes.

"Rance told some reporter she was here," one of them said. "We did try to reason with him, Mr. Nelson, but he was half lit and out for blood. Dale Branigan fed him a lot of bull about you and he's sweet on her; not to mention him drinking like a fish half the time when you didn't see him."

"He can be sweet on her from a closer distance from now on," Gene said, trying to cope with all the new developments at once. He'd been lax on the job a lot. It was just coming home to him how much time he'd spent wallowing in self-pity over his parentage while he let his stepfather's ranch go to hell. Well, there wouldn't be any more of that. He stood over Rance, watching the man open a swollen eye to stare up at him with evident fear.

"Get off my land," Gene said coldly, and without raising his voice. "If I see you again, I'll break your neck. I'll send your check along in care of Dale Branigan. But if you're counting on a little romance with her, you'll have to get past Ben Hardy. He's all but engaged to her, in case you didn't know."

Rance looked shocked. "Ben...?"

"She played you for a fool, didn't she?" Gene asked with a mocking smile. "You poor stupid fish, that will be all over town by tomorrow, too. I promise you it will, along with the news of my engagement to Allison and the damage you tried to do to her reputation."

Rance dragged himself to his feet, considerably more sober now. He wiped blood away from a cut lip and shivered a little with reaction and muscle strain as he reached for his hat and put it back on.

"No need to beat a man half to death over some woman," Rance said angrily.

"No need to make her out to be a tramp because she won't let you touch her, either," Gene said dangerously, his temper kindling again. "You're finished in Pryor, Rance. I'll see to it, no matter what it takes."

Rance straightened. "I've had my fill of Wyoming, anyway," he said shortly. "You can have it."

He hobbled into the bunkhouse to pack. Gene turned on his heel and walked away, ignoring the murmurs of comment from his men as he stalked toward the house with blood in his eye.

He went straight up the staircase without a word to Marie and Winnie, who'd been standing speechless at the window, watching the byplay.

Dwight was asleep when he peeped in the door, so he went straight along to Allison's room.

He knocked and waited for her to answer. It only took a minute. She was surprised to see him, and he wondered absently if she'd have opened it if she'd known it was him. She looked terrible.

He rubbed his fist against the corner of his mouth, feeling the cut there as he stared down at her furiously. "Why didn't you tell me what Rance was saying about you?" he demanded without preamble. "Why didn't you tell me what you'd gone through in Central America, and what you and your parents were doing there?"

She was looking at his bruised, cut face, hardly hearing the words. "You're hurt," she said worriedly. "What happened to you?"

"I've been out in the backyard beating the hell out of Rance before I fired him," he said icily. "And I enjoyed it. Does that shock you? I wish I'd hit him twice as damned hard!"

"You know...all of it?" she asked hesitantly.

"All of it," he assured her. His broad chest rose and fell jerkily. "Oh, God, why didn't you trust me?" he asked huskily. "Why didn't you tell me the truth?"

Her eyes fell to his shirt buttons. "I couldn't. It hurt too much to talk about it, at first. And then I knew you'd take off like a shot if you knew, well, what I did for a living. I lied because I wanted to be alive, just for a little while. I wanted to be someone else, I wanted to be like other women, to be...loved." She almost choked on the word and her eyes closed. "But I had no right."

"Do you think I did?" he groaned. He stepped into the room and slammed the door, jerking her hungrily into his arms. He held her against him, rocking her gently, folding her to his heart in a silence that was broken only by the sound of her soft weeping.

"The worst of it is that I was so wrapped up in my own problems that I was blind to your character," he said bitterly. "I deliberately overlooked all the telltale signs of your innocence because I wanted you so badly. I deserve to be shot!"

"But, I wanted you, too," she whispered at his ear, feeling his cheek warm and rough against hers as he held her. "It's not all your fault. You were hurting. I understood."

"That doesn't excuse it. And to have that redheaded vermin gossiping about you in town!'' he groaned. ''I'm sorry.''

''I won't be here much longer,'' she reminded him miserably. ''And if that reporter just doesn't find me...''

His arms tightened. ''It won't matter if he does,'' he said curtly. ''I've just told the men that we're engaged. I'll make sure that gets around town. Dale will wind up with egg on her face from her damned gossiping.''

''Engaged?'' she gasped. ''But I can't!''

He drew back, scowling. ''Why can't you? You're a missionary, not a nun. Marriage is permissible.''

''But not like this, Gene,'' she said quietly, her hazel eyes sad and regretful. ''Not to spare my reputation. It will be all right. I'm a qualified nurse. I can still get a job.''

His eyes searched her face, down to her soft mouth. ''Marriage is a job, isn't it? Dwight and I are switching responsibilities, and we'll both be happier. That means I'll be home more. I can spend time with you and the kids.''

She flushed. ''There aren't any kids.''

His lean hands smoothed down her hips and one of them lightly touched her belly. ''Yet.''

She shivered and tried to pull away.

But he held her, gently, firmly. ''I know. I hurt you, didn't I? Your first time was a nightmare that you don't want to repeat, especially with me.''

She nodded slowly, without looking at him.

He bent and suddenly lifted her in his hard arms,

his eyes searching her frightened ones as he carried her toward the bed.

"If I can make you want me, in spite of what happened before, will you agree to marry me?" he asked softly.

"But, I don't...!" she protested.

He covered the frantic words with his mouth, gently this time, using every shred of skill he possessed to coax her set lips into a shy response.

He laid her down on the coverlet and stretched out beside her, his lips teasing hers in a gentle, exquisite kind of exploration. His fingers traced her cheeks, pushing back the wispy strands of long black hair that had escaped from her bun while the seconds lengthened into minutes.

"I like your hair long and loose," he breathed against her yielding mouth, one lean hand disposing of pins and combs before he arranged her loosened mane of hair around her flushed face.

She looked up at him nervously, her body already taut from the threat of his, her memory all too vivid of the last time.

"There's a barrier," he whispered deeply, holding her eyes while he traced a long forefinger around the swollen contours of her mouth. "It's called a maidenhead. It protects a woman's chastity. The first time, it has to be disposed of, and that's why I hurt you. It won't ever be like that again. Now that I know how innocent you really are, I'll make a meal of you, Miss Hathoway. When I've finished, fear is the last thing you'll feel when you look at me."

She colored. "I'm a nurse," she reminded him,

trying to sound worldly. "I do know something about my own anatomy."

He brushed her open mouth with his. "I was in too much of a hurry to wait for you. I lost my head. I won't lose it with you again until I've satisfied you."

"Please," she moaned, "you mustn't talk to me like this!"

"You're my woman," he said, lifting his head to hold her eyes. "We're lovers, Allison. We're going to be married. You'll have to face the implications of that, sooner or later."

"I won't marry you!"

"Like hell you won't marry me," he said with quiet determination. He searched her eyes. "I'm sorry," he said as he bent. "But this is the only way, now."

She didn't understand what he meant at first. He covered her mouth with his and his hands smoothed down her body while he built the kiss from a slow caress to a blazing, raging statement of intent. She shivered as the heat exploded in her body when his mouth suddenly went down hard over her breast and began to suckle it through the fabric of her dress. She arched and gasped, at the same time that one lean hand found the fastening of her jeans and slipped expertly inside against warm flesh.

"Gene, you can't!" she whimpered.

But he touched her intimately then, and his mouth became as insistent and rhythmic as the hand invading her privacy with such slow, sweet mastery. She began to shiver. Her eyes closed. She couldn't fight this sweet tide of pleasure, she couldn't! She heard her breath shuddering out in little gasps, felt her body lifting, yielding itself to whatever he wanted. His face nuzzled under the fabric of her blouse and nudged her bra aside so that he could find the hard, aching tip of her swelling breast, hot and moist against the silky bare flesh.

"Gene," she whispered, her voice breaking on his name as he quickened the rhythm and increased the insistence of his mouth on her body. "Gene! Oh, Gene, please—!"

Her voice broke and he gave her what she begged for, feeling her release with pride and indulgent pleasure. He lifted his head and watched her convulse, her face a study in rigid ecstasy, her body completely his. She wept afterward, and he comforted her, kissing away the tears, lightly caressing her trembling body until she was completely still in his arms.

"That's what it feels like, Allison," he said softly, holding her shocked eyes. "That's what it was like for me, that night in the cabin. I wanted you to know, because next time, I'll give you this same pleasure with my body. Only it will be an agony of a climax, I promise you. This will be nothing by comparison."

She blushed as she met his eyes. "Why?"

He kissed her nose. "I told you. I want you to marry me."

"You don't have to go that far to spare my reputation, or salve your own guilt. I told you, I don't blame you...Gene!" she gasped sharply.

His body had levered over hers in midsentence and he'd coaxed his way between her long legs, so that she felt him in blatant intimacy, became shockingly aware of the power and need of his body.

He moved deliberately, balancing himself above her on his forearms, smiling down at her with the slow, deliberate shifting of his lean hips.

"Say, yes, I'll marry you, Gene," he instructed very slowly, "or I'll peel you out of those jeans right now and make you scream like a banshee under me. If you think your reputation's in shreds already, wait until that unholy crew in the bunkhouse hears the noises I drag out of you now."

She shivered, because she was vulnerable and he knew it. Worse, the window was open, she glanced at it and saw the curtains moving.

"Better say it quick, cupcake, before I get too involved to roll away," he said huskily and pressed his lips down hard over hers. "It's getting worse."

Yes, it was, and her face registered her knowledge of it. She swallowed, sensations in her lower belly making her hot and weak all at once. Her legs trembled under his. "You can't do that...to me," she protested. "Marie and Winnie—"

"Are downstairs," he said, "and the door is closed. Neither of them is likely to walk in without an invitation since they know I'm up here with you," he said in a deep, husky tone. "Open your legs, Allison," he whispered, his mouth poising over hers to brush at it with soft, sensual intent. His own long, powerful legs began to edge out and she felt him against her in a hot daze. She gasped softly and looked up into his glittering green eyes, feeling a kindred recklessness. With a faint moan, she let him shift her legs, let him fit his lean body intimately to hers while he watched her face with unblinking intensity. His jaw tautened and she felt his body swell even more in the stark closeness. She shivered.

His hand went between them and ripped open his shirt and pushed hers up, easily unclipping her bra and moving it out of the way. He looked down as he brushed his hair-roughened chest blatantly over the hard tips of her breasts and watched her shiver with reaction. His hips began to move upward over hers, throbbing with building passion as his eyes bit into hers.

"Tell me you don't want to be filled," he whispered at her lips. "Filled hard, and deep."

She made a helpless sound and shivered again, totally helpless.

His hands went to her jeans, and then to his own, and seconds later, she felt his muscular, hair-roughened nudity against her softness with a sense of wonder. His body echoed the soft shiver of hers.

"Are you going to let me?" he whispered, drawing his hips against hers.

"We shouldn't...Gene," she choked.

"Yes, we should," he whispered tenderly. His hands smoothed down her silky hips, under her thighs, and he lifted them, eased them apart with such gentleness that she couldn't find a single protest.

He moved then, fitting himself to her in a silence that smoldered with promise.

She looked straight into his eyes and gasped softly as he began to possess her, with exquisitely gentle movements.

"Yes," he whispered tenderly. "You see? It doesn't hurt. No, don't tense up. That's it," he coaxed. He took her mouth under his and cherished it. "That's it, little one. I'm only going to love you. Isn't that what you said you wanted? To be loved?"

She'd meant another kind of love entirely, but this was heaven. She wondered if he'd ever been so tender with anyone else, but he moved then, and she couldn't think anymore.

He probed her body softly. "Yes, watch my eyes, Allison. You watched me, that night. Now I want to watch you."

As he spoke, he moved, slow and easy movements that brought them first into stark intimacy, and then into contact, and then totally together. She gasped as she felt her body absorbing his, stunned with the ease of his passage, the readiness of her own body. She stared into his eyes with wonder, trying to feel guilt and shame, but she couldn't. She couldn't have imagined the expression on his lean face in her wildest dreams. His eyes were soft and warm, full of secret knowledge and tenderness and excitement.

He moved lazily against her, smiling as he settled on her body in a soft rhythm that lifted her very slowly to an ecstasy she'd never dreamed possible.

She cried out and pushed at his chest, frightened, but he continued the steady rhythm, increasing it now, his breathing suddenly changing as he watched her eyes.

"Don't look away," he said huskily. "I'm going to watch. Now, Allison. Now, little one. Now. Now!"

She made sounds she'd never made in her life as

the sensations gathered and suddenly exploded. She wept in what sounded like anguished pain, her breath trapped in her throat, her face contorted like her convulsing body. He went with her every step of the way, only giving in when she was almost exhausted. He laughed even as his body corded over hers, laughed through the vicious ecstasy that suspended him above her in a shuddering anguish of satisfaction.

He ground out something and went rigid before he collapsed on her body, his heartbeat shaking both of them. He trembled, as she did, long afterward.

"I really should have closed the window," he murmured dryly, feeling the heat in her cheeks. "Don't curl up. We're too far from the bunkhouse and the living room for anyone to hear you, and Dwight's asleep. Did it hurt this time?" he asked, smiling as he lifted his head to search her eyes, knowing the answer already.

She swallowed. "Oh, no," she whispered. She was still trembling a little, and so was he. They were both drenched with sweat, but her body felt deliciously boneless, although it still tingled with pleasure. "No, it was…" She searched for the right word as she looked into his soft eyes. "It was beautiful."

"That's how it should be," he breathed at her ear, gathering her legs in the muscular cage of his as he kissed her tenderly. He lifted his head. "I hope you weren't disappointed this time."

"You were…watching," she whispered, coloring. "Couldn't you, well, see?"

"I saw, all right." His face hardened with the memory and he kissed her roughly. "I've never watched before. I've never been satisfied like that before, either. If you don't marry me, so help me, I'll move in here with you until I shame you into saying yes.''

She swallowed. "Gene..."

He brushed back her damp hair. "Your conscience will beat you to death over this," he said quietly, drawing her gaze along their bodies until she flushed and averted her eyes. "I didn't force you or coerce you. It was mutual. We've got a lot going for us. I want to live with you, cupcake.''

"Sex wouldn't be enough for you," she whispered sadly. "And you'd have a long time to regret it.''

"I won't regret it." He brushed his mouth over her eyes. And he knew he wouldn't. He was awash with new feelings, with a tenderness he'd never experienced before. He studied her quietly. "You'll be everything I ever needed, or wanted. I'll take care of you until I die. And someday, somehow, I'll make you glad you said yes.''

Those words echoed in her mind long after they'd dressed and gone downstairs to announce their engagement. Allison couldn't decide if she believed him or not; if she dared to believe him. Because it sounded very much as if more than physical need was the basis for the proposal. About that, only time would tell.

Ten

"**I** just can't believe it," Marie said later, smiling at Allison. "I never thought I'd live long enough to see Gene married. Imagine that, my footloose, fancy-free brother not only willing, but anxious to tie the knot! And to someone I really like!"

"I'm glad of that," Allison said, but her eyes were troubled.

Winnie was upstairs with Dwight, and Gene had gone back out to work after a brief lunch. Marie was still getting over the shock of what Gene had announced so matter-of-factly.

Marie stared at her for a moment. "There's something more, isn't there?" she asked gently. "Forgive me for prying, but I know my brother very well and I've learned quite a bit about you. Something happened that night that Rance gossiped about, and you think Gene is only marrying you to appease his conscience. That's it, isn't it?"

Allison started to deny it, but there really wasn't any point. She stared down at her hands folded in her lap. "Yes."

"Gene has a conscience," Marie continued. "But nothing could make him marry a woman in cold blood, not even that. You'd better believe that it isn't guilt on his part."

"There could be a baby," Allison said painfully, amazed that she could talk to Marie this way when she couldn't bring herself to tell Winnie about it.

Marie smiled. "Gene loves children," she said simply. "So do all the rest of us. A baby would be the sweetest kind of surprise."

Allison fought tears and lost. She put her head in her hands and wept bitterly. "I've trapped him, all because I got in over my head," she moaned. "Whatever his motives, inevitably he'll hate me!"

Marie hugged her warmly. "No, I don't think so. Not the way he's been acting since you've been around. You've changed him. All the bitterness and mockery are gone. He's gentler, less volatile."

"Mr. Rance wouldn't agree with you," Allison said with a watery smile.

"Mr. Rance deserved what he got," Marie said shortly. "I don't feel sorry for him. Now you cheer up," she told Allison. "No more regrets. You're the first sister-in-law prospect Gene's ever presented me with, and I'm not letting you escape!"

Marie's enthusiasm was catching. Allison went

back up to sit with Dwight in a brighter mood altogether. If she had doubts, she kept them to herself.

Gene led her off into the study later that night, after they'd had supper, and closed the door.

She was nervous, and he smiled gently at the expression on her face.

"Don't look so threatened," he said, his green eyes twinkling at her. "The couch is too short, and the desk would be hell on your back."

She blushed, her eyes like saucers as they met his.

He moved toward her, indulgent and smiling. "How can you still blush?" he asked, drawing her gently to him. "You wide-eyed little innocent."

"Not so innocent now," she said quietly.

He bent and kissed her softly. "It won't do much good to ask you not to beat your conscience to death. But try not to go overboard. God made us human, little one," he said, his voice deep and caressing as he searched her eyes. "He gave us physical pleasure to insure the perpetuation of the species."

"And He gave us responsibility not to make a mockery of it, or twist it into something bad," she replied miserably.

He framed her wan face in his lean hands and studied her. "You believed in me when no one else did," he said. "You weren't put off by my reputation or intimidated by my temper. You gave yourself to me more than any other reason because you knew how desperately I needed you." He sighed heavily. "Allison, what we did, that night at the cabin and today, was as natural as breathing. It isn't hateful to want someone, especially when it goes beyond a physical need.''

"Did it, though?" she asked sadly.

He nodded. "Yes. This afternoon, it most certainly went beyond desire."

"You were...so tender," she whispered.

He drew her against him and enveloped her in his arms, resting his cheek on her dark hair. "It's going to be that way every time, from now on," he said. His arms tightened as he felt her warmth and softness so close to him. His body reacted predictably and he laughed. "My God, feel that," he whispered at her ear.

"Stop," she protested in a flutter.

"You're a nurse. You should know that I can't stop it."

"That wasn't what I meant." She buried her face in his chest and felt him suddenly go stiff and catch his breath.

His hands moved slowly into her hair. He drew her mouth against him, through the shirt, and his breathing became ragged. "Allison," he whispered huskily. His eyes closed. He'd never felt so vulnerable, or minded it so little.

"You like that?" she whispered hesitantly.

"I like it a lot." He eased a lean hand between them. "But I'd like it on my bare skin more, sweetheart," he said, unfastening buttons as he spoke. "Push my shirt out of the way and put your mouth on me," he whispered sensuously.

"We shouldn't," she protested weakly. "What if..."

"We're going to be married," he said at her forehead. "A piece of paper and the right words aren't
going to bind us any closer than our bodies already
have. You're mine now. I love being part of you,
feeling you share my pleasure. Is it really so frightening to let me love you now?"

"It isn't...frightening," she confessed. She rubbed
her hands flat against his hair-laden chest, up and
down in a sensual pattern.

He drew her mouth to his warm skin, feeling her
lips search through the mat of hair to the hard muscles
of his chest and he caught his breath, tautening involuntarily.

It was intoxicating, she thought dazedly, smoothing
her hands over him while her mouth lifted and
touched. He smelled of spicy cologne and the touch
of his body was all of heaven.

Her hands smoothed down to his belt and his lips
brushed her closed eyelids. "Lower," he whispered.
"I want you to touch me."

She hesitated. She was curious, but all her inhibitions were protesting.

"I belong to you as surely as you belong to me,"
he said quietly. "Aren't you curious about the differ-
ences between your body and mine?"

"Well, yes," she confessed hesitantly.

His lips parted against her eyebrows. "Then find
them out for yourself."

She lay her cheek on his chest and slowly let her
cool, nervous hands trespass past the wide belt. He
jerked a little at the unfamiliar touch, and she hesi-

tated, but his hands trapped hers when she tried to pull them away.

"It's all right," he whispered against her temple. "I'm no more used to this than you are."

"You're experienced..." she protested.

"Not in this, I'm not," he replied, surprisingly. "What we've done together is totally new for me, up to and including this. Haven't you realized that I'm not playing some sophisticated game with you?" he asked. "Allison, I'm as helpless as you are when we make love. Your touch is just as exciting and potent to me as mine seems to be to you."

"I didn't realize that," she whispered. Under her softly questing hands, his body was powerfully male and very, very responsive. He gasped and she felt his body shudder. "Did I hurt you?" she breathed.

"No," he said, his voice faintly choked. "I'm sensitive there."

"Oh."

"Don't stop," he whispered, searching for her lips with his mouth. He opened it to a slow, deep kiss that seemed to have no end, glorying in her tender exploration of him. He guided her hand to the zipper and groaned helplessly when she touched him under the fabric. They wound up on the couch in a tangle of arms and legs, fighting their way into each others' arms through a sea of uncooperative clothing.

She shivered, her breasts flattened in the thicket of hair on his warm chest, swelling as he traced them with his thumbs while they kissed.

"When are you going to marry me?" he whispered into her open mouth.

"Whenever...you like," she managed unsteadily. "Friday?"

"That's only three days away," she said huskily.

He smiled against her mouth. "I know." He lifted his head and looked down where her body was lying across his lap, her torso bare against his. "And not a minute too soon." He tugged at her lower lip with his teeth, in a sensual throbbing fantasy that made him dizzy. "Make a baby with me, Allison," he whispered, easing her down onto the sofa as he lifted his head to hold her hazel eyes in thrall. "Here. Now."

"Gene...!" she exclaimed when he moved.

But it was already too late for second thoughts, because he joined them with a minimum of fuss and smiled gently into her shocked eyes as he began to move sensually and with expert knowledge of her body.

"Yes, that's it," he whispered when she ground her teeth together and gasped. "Only don't cry out when I satisfy you," he added with a slow, sensual smile, "because the walls aren't that thick and the door isn't locked. Do you hear me? Bite my chest or kiss me when it happens, so that the sound doesn't penetrate the walls. God, you're noisy," he whispered as she began to bite back the sounds. "One day I'll make love to you deep in the woods and you can scream for me. Yes. Yes. That's it, lift up to me." His hands gripped her hips and pulled her to him in a ragged, rough rhythm. "Yes. Yes!" His eyes closed and he began to shudder, then they opened straight into hers and his body impaled her fiercely. She felt the spiraling rhythm explode into ecstasy and racked her slender body.

"I want a son!" he bit off in her ear, and his hands clenched on her hips and ground her into him as he shuddered against her.

It was the most unbelievable pleasure she'd ever shared with him. She wept bitterly when he collapsed against her, clinging to him and trembling in the aftermath.

"God, that was good," he whispered hoarsely at her ear. His arms contracted, riveting her to him. "Did you hear what I said, just at the last?"

"Yes." She drew him closer. "You whispered that you wanted a son," she said, shivering.

"I meant it. A son. A daughter. Our child." He lifted his head and searched her eyes, his sweaty hair hanging down onto his broad forehead, his green eyes glittery with spent pleasure. "It's exciting to make love like this. I never wanted children before. But it's all I think about when I'm with you."

She reached up and touched his mouth. "I can never say no to you," she whispered. "It's... frightening."

"It's your inhibitions," he corrected. He kissed her softly and moved away, smiling indulgently at her embarrassment as she rearranged her clothing while he fastened his own. "Feverish, isn't it?" he asked wickedly. "Hot and wild and out of control. You're every dream I ever dreamed. I don't know how I lived this long without you."

"Are you sure it isn't just physical?" she asked after a minute, really worried.

He brought her face up to his and kissed her gently. "If it was only physical, why would I want to make babies with you?" he whispered tenderly.

She smiled, her heart in her eyes, and laid her head against his chest. "Then I'll marry you whenever you say, Gene."

He hesitated. "There's something I have to tell you, before you commit yourself," he told her a minute later. "A secret I've held back. I should have told you before we ever got involved. I can't ask you to live with me unless you know it."

She lifted her head. "It won't matter. What is it?"

"My father," he began slowly, watching her face closely, "my real father, I mean…is in prison."

Her eyes didn't waver. She smiled up at him. "I'm sorry about that. But what does it have to do with my marrying you?"

He let out the breath he'd been holding. "My God," he ground out. He caught her up roughly and held her close enough to bruise her, his eyes closed as he rocked her against him. "My God, I was scared to death to tell you…!"

"But why?" she asked gently.

"You might be afraid of our children inheriting bad blood," he said curtly. "My father is a thief. From what I've been able to find out, he's been in trouble with the law all his life."

She nuzzled her face against him, feeling warm and safe and secure. "Environment plays a big part in shaping a person's character," she said drowsily. "I get sleepy when you love me. Is that natural?"

His breath caught. "When I love you," he repeated

in a slow whisper, feeling the words to his bones. His eyes closed and he held her closer, shivering. Love her. Love her. It *was* loving. Why hadn't he realized it? "My God."

"Is something wrong?" she asked, her voice puzzled.

"No. Not a single thing." He drew back and searched her eyes, holding them while he looked for more secrets, hoping that he'd hit on the right one. "How do you feel about me, sweetheart?" he asked gently.

"I...I want you," she stammered, embarrassed.

He shook his head slowly. "Sex wouldn't be enough for you. Even good sex. Not with your background. Try again."

She hesitated. It was hard to lay her heart down in front of him, but clearly that was what he wanted.

He brushed his thumb over her soft lips. "It takes a lot of trust, doesn't it? But I trusted you enough to tell you the most painful secret I have."

That was true. He had. She was the one lacking in trust, not him. She drew a slow, steadying breath and looked up at him. "I love you, Gene," she said simply.

"Do you?" he asked huskily.

The expression on his lean, hard face made her confident. "With all my heart," she whispered.

He traced the soft contours of her mouth with fingers that were faintly unsteady. "Forever, little one," he breathed, bending to her mouth.

Tears stung her eyes as she closed them. "Forever!"

He kissed her with aching tenderness and picked her up in his arms, sitting down in an armchair with her in his lap. He tucked her face into his throat and sat just holding her close for a long, long time before he finally leaned back with a heavy sigh to light a cigarette, still cradling her close.

"Now, you're going to tell me about your parents."

She shivered. "I can't."

"You can. We're part of each other now. There's nothing you can't share with me. Tell me about them."

She lay quietly for a minute. Then she began to speak. She told him about the countries where they'd lived, the conditions of unspeakable poverty they'd endured.

"They never let it get them down," she told him. "They were always sure that things would get better. If we ran out of supplies, they were confident that new ones would come in time. And they always did," she said wonderingly. "I've never known people like them. They really lived what they believed in. And then, one day, it all came down around our ears. The regimes changed so quickly." She hesitated.

He pulled her closer, sensing her feelings. "I've got you. You're safe. Tell me what happened."

"We were arrested for giving comfort to the enemy," she said, giving in to the terrifying memories. She pressed closer. "They locked us up overnight. Even then, my parents were sure that we'd be set free by the government troops when they arrived. But the next morning we were marched out of the village along with some other political prisoners and stood up against an ocotillo fence.'' She swallowed. ''We could hear firing in the distance. I kept thinking, if we can just hold on for a few minutes, they'll come, they'll rescue us. Just as I thought it, the guns started firing. My father, and then my mother, fell beside me. I closed my eyes, waiting.'' She shivered and he held her close, bruisingly close. ''A bullet whizzed past my head and I knew the next one was going to get me. But before it hit, gunfire erupted around the three of us who were still alive. I was taken out of the village by a priest we knew. He got me to safety, although how is still a blur. I got to the American Embassy and they put me on a plane back to the United States. Of all the people I knew, Winnie was the only one I could trust, so I called her and she brought me here.''

He thanked God that she was with him, that he was holding her, that the bullets had missed and the soldiers had saved her. ''So that's why you came here.''

She nodded, staring across his broad chest toward the window. She sighed heavily. ''It was a nightmare. Sometimes I still wake up crying in the night.''

''If you wake up crying from now on, I'll be there to hold you,'' he said gently. ''Starting tonight.''

''But, Gene…!''

He put a finger over her lips. ''I'll leave you before morning. No one will know except the two of us.'' He searched her soft eyes. ''God, honey, it's going to be hell being separated from you even while I work, much less at night, do you know that? I don't want you out of my sight!''

Her lips parted on a rush of breath.

"Are you shocked?" he asked huskily, searching her rapt face. "I thought you knew by now that I'm hopelessly in love with you, Allie."

"Oh, Gene," she whispered, shaken.

"I never knew what love was," he said softly. "I'm not sure I was even alive until you came along."

"I feel the same way," she whispered. Her fingers touched his hard mouth tenderly. "I'd die for you, Gene."

His eyes closed and he shivered. He'd never felt anything so intense, or so special.

Allison kissed him softly, again and again. He looked as if he needed comforting. Incredible, for such an independent, self-sufficient man.

"What about your career, little one?" he asked later.

"I can't go back to it," she murmured, without mentioning the blemish on her reputation from the night in the line cabin that would cost her that career. There was no need to make him feel worse than he already did. "I couldn't ask you to leave here and follow me around the world. And I couldn't go without you. Besides," she said gently, "there's every possibility that I could be pregnant now. Today was the very best time for it to happen."

"Was it?" he murmured, and smiled tenderly, laying a big, lean hand on her belly. "Kids and cattle sort of go together, you know. It takes a big family to manage these days."

"I'd like a big family," she said drowsily, curling up in his hard arms. "I hope we can have one."

"If we can't, there are plenty of kids around who'd love to be needed by someone," he murmured, smiling. "Raising them makes people parents, not just having them."

She smiled back. "I'm sleepy."

His arms contracted. "Too much loving," he whispered. "I've exhausted you."

She opened her eyes and looked up at him. "Only temporarily," she whispered. "I love how it feels with you when you love me, Gene."

His jaw tensed. "So do I." He drew in a steadying breath. "We'd better get out of here before it happens again. You make me insatiable."

"I hope to keep you that way, when we're married," she said shyly.

"I'll hold you to it," he promised. He lifted her and got up, too. "I have something for you. In the heat of things, I forgot to give it to you." He opened his desk drawer and removed a felt-covered box. He opened it and slid a marquise diamond onto her engagement finger, leaving the companion wedding band in the box.

"Do you want me to wear a ring when we're married?" he asked seriously.

"Of course," she replied. "If I wear your brand," she said with a mischievous smile, "you have to wear mine."

He chuckled. "Nelson's brand, is that it? I like the sound of it. No trespassing allowed."

"And don't you forget it," she said.

She clung to his hand, wonderingly, astonished that her life could have changed so much in such a short period of time. All her nightmares were going to fade away now, she was sure of it.

Gene was equally sure of it. He'd laid his own ghosts to rest, including his worst one. Allison had said that environment played a big part in shaping a man's character. Perhaps it did. Maybe his real father had had a hard time of it and couldn't cope. Whatever the reason, it didn't have to affect his own life unless he let it. He could live with being an adopted Nelson. Marie and Dwight loved him, there was no doubt about that, and he and Dwight were going to work out the rest of the problems. He'd never been so certain of anything. He looked down at Allison and felt as if he were floating.

Dwight was able to go to the wedding the following week. He and Marie and Winnie witnessed at the small, quiet ceremony where Allison Hathoway became Mrs. Gene Nelson. She wore a simple white dress and carried a bouquet of daisies, and Gene thought he'd never seen anyone so beautiful. He said so, several times after they arrived at the hotel in Yellowstone National Park where they were spending part of their honeymoon.

"The most amazing thing is that nobody discovered we were sharing a bed until we got married," Allison said with a shy smile.

"Sharing it was all we did," he murmured ruefully, "because of your conscience. Not to mention my own. But it was sweet, honey. I never dreamed anything could be as sweet as holding you all night in my arms, even if we didn't make love.''

''And now we never have to be apart again,'' she whispered, lifting into his arms as he began to kiss her very softly.

''Did you notice the reporter?'' he asked against her mouth.

''The one you sent sprawling into the mud puddle?'' she whispered, laughing involuntarily when she remembered the astonishment on the journalist's face. ''Amazing that he finally found me, and by the time he did, it didn't matter anymore. They've started releasing all sorts of information through the international forces. I'm old news now.''

''Thank God. He won't be hounding us anymore.''

''I just wish my parents could have gotten out with me,'' she said, allowing herself that one regret.

''So do I, little one,'' he replied gently. ''I'm just glad that you did.''

She pressed close to him, drawing strength from his lean, powerful body.

''Make love to me this time,'' he whispered at her ear.

''But I don't know how,'' she said softly.

''No problem. I'll teach you.''

And he did. He guided her, smiled at her reticence, laughed at her fumbling efforts to undress him. But when they were finally together on the big bed, softness to hardness, dark to light, the laughing stopped and they loved as they never had before. From tenderness to rough passion, to lazy sweetness and sharp demand, they didn't sleep all night long. By morning they lay exhausted in each others' arms, too tired to even move.

It was lunchtime before they stirred. Allison opened her eyes to find Gene sitting on the bed beside her, watching her as he toweled his hair dry.

"Good morning, Mrs. Nelson," he said softly.

She opened her arms, smiling as she dislodged the sheet and felt him lift her against his bare chest while he kissed her tenderly.

"Was it good?" he whispered.

"I thought I was going to die," she replied huskily.

"So did I. And I still may." He groaned, sitting upright, and then he laughed. "I think my back's broken."

"Married twenty-four hours, and you're already complaining," she moaned.

"That wasn't a complaint," he chuckled. He kissed her again and pulled her out of bed, his eyes sliding possessively over her soft pink nudity. "God, you're beautiful. Inside and out. You're my world, Allison."

She pressed close against him. "You're mine. I'll never live long enough to tell you how much I love you."

"Yes, you will." He smoothed her hair. "Now get dressed. I don't know about you, but I'm starved!"

"Come to think of it, so am I," she said, blinking. "Gene, we never had supper! Not to mention breakfast or lunch!"

He chuckled. "We didn't, did we?"

"No wonder we're hungry!"

"Amen. So get moving, woman."

She got dressed, with his dubious assistance, which

took twice as long. They had a leisurely supper and then went out to see Old Faithful erupt. Later they drove up to the mud volcano, past the fishing bridge, and sat beside a little stream that cut through towering lodgepole pines with the jagged Rocky Mountains rising majestically in the distance and Yellowstone Lake in the other direction.

"Tomorrow's Sunday," he said when they were back in the hotel room, curled up together in bed.

"So it is," she replied.

He sighed softly and pressed her cheek to his bare chest. "They have church services nearby," he said. "I asked. Suppose we go?"

Her breath caught. She sat up, looking at him in the light from outside the room. "Do you mean it? You really want to?"

"I mean it," he said quietly.

She had to fight tears. "Oh, Gene," she whispered, because she knew what a giant step it was for him to make.

He brushed away the moistness from her eyes. "I love you," he said. "From now on, we go together—wherever we go."

"Yes." She laughed, so full of happiness that it was all but overflowing. "Oh, yes!"

He pulled her close and rested his cheek on her soft hair. Minutes later, he heard her breathing change as she fell asleep. He watched her sleeping face with quiet wonder for a few minutes before he pulled the covers over them and settled down beside her, with her cheek resting on his broad, warm shoulder.

Outside, a bird was making soft night noises, and

his eyes closed as he relaxed into the mattress. He'd been looking for a place in life, somewhere he belonged, somewhere he fit. Now he'd found it. He fit very nicely into Allison's warm, soft arms—and even better in her gentle heart. She made him complete. He closed his eyes with a slow smile. He'd have to remember to tell her that in the morning.

* * * * * *

They called her the

Champagne Girl

Catherine: Underneath the effervescent, carefree and bubbly
facade there was a depth to which few
had access.

Matt: The older stepbrother she inherited with her
mother's second marriage, Matt continually
complicated things. It seemed to Catherine that
she would make plans only to have Matt foul
them up.

With the perfect job waiting in New York City, only one thing
would be able to keep her on a dusty cattle ranch: something
she thought she could never have—the love of the sexiest
cowboy in the Lone Star state.

by bestselling author

DIANA PALMER

Available in September 1997 at your favorite retail outlet.

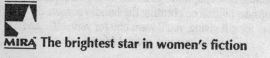

<u>**MIRA**</u> **The brightest star in women's fiction**   MDP8

Look us up on-line at: http://www.romance.net

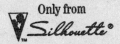

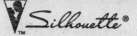
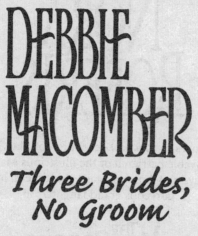

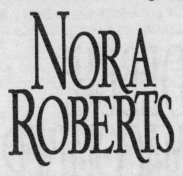

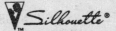

FANTASTIC NEWS!

For all you devoted Diana Palmer fans
Silhouette Books is pleased to bring you
a brand-new novel and short story by one of the
top ten romance writers in America

"Nobody tops Diana Palmer...I love her stories."
—*New York Times* bestselling author
Jayne Ann Krentz

Diana Palmer has written another thrilling desire.
Man of the Month Ramon Cortero was a talented
surgeon, existing only for his work—until the
night he saved nurse Noreen Kensington's life. But
their stormy past makes this romance a challenge!

THE PATIENT NURSE
Silhouette Desire
October 1997

And in November Diana Palmer adds to the
Long, Tall Texans series with *CHRISTMAS COWBOY*, in
LONE STAR CHRISTMAS, a fabulous new holiday
keepsake collection by talented authors Diana Palmer
and Joan Johnston. Their heroes are seductive,
shameless and irresistible—and these Texans are
experts at sneaking kisses under the mistletoe! So get
ready for a sizzling holiday season....

Only from ▼ᵀᴹ *Silhouette*®